SAXBY SMART
PRIVATE DETECTIVE

The *Saxby Smart – Private Detective* series:

The Curse of the Ancient Mask and other case files
The Fangs of the Dragon and other case files
The Pirate's Blood and other case files

Coming soon:
The Eye of the Serpent and other case files
Five Seconds to Doomsday and other case files

Solve another Saxby mystery,
exclusively online at:

www.piccadillypress.co.uk/saxbysmart

SAXBY SMART
PRIVATE DETECTIVE

THE HANGMAN'S LAIR

AND OTHER CASE FILES

SIMON CHESHIRE

Piccadilly Press • London

First published in Great Britain in 2008
by Piccadilly Press Ltd,
5 Castle Road, London NW1 8PR
www.piccadillypress.co.uk

A catalogue record for this book is available
from the British Library

ISBN: 978 1 85340 994 3 (paperback)

1 3 5 7 9 10 8 6 4 2

Printed in the UK by CPI Bookmarque, Croydon CR0 4TD
Cover design by Fielding Design

Introduction: Important Facts

My name is Saxby Smart and I'm a private detective. I go to St Egbert's School, my office is in the garden shed, and this is the fourth book of my case files. Unlike some detectives, I don't have a sidekick, so that part I'm leaving up to you – pay attention, I'll ask questions.

Case File Ten:

The Hangman's Lair

Chapter One

SOMETIMES IT'S FAR FROM EASY being a brilliant schoolboy detective like me. After a while, you get a reputation around school for being able to solve any mystery, no matter how strange or mind-mangling.

So I was very embarrassed when *The Mystery of the Money Stolen From the School Office* left me completely clueless. Half of St Egbert's School was keeping a close eye on me as I examined the scene of the crime and talked to possible suspects. The pressure on me to get a result was made even worse by the fact that the headteacher had only allowed me to investigate once the police had been called in and *they'd* been left clueless too.

It was like this: a wad of cash, totalling four hundred and twenty pounds, had been sitting on the school secretary's desk at lunchtime on Monday. This money had been collected from pupils, and was going to pay for a school trip that all of my year group had been looking forward to.

The secretary, Mrs McEwan, had been in the office the whole time. She'd turned away from her desk for about ten seconds (to thump the computer's very expensive printer to get it working, she told me quietly, but shh, don't tell anyone, especially the Head). When she turned back, the money was gone.

She'd run out into the corridor. Nobody in sight. She'd searched the office. Nothing had fallen off her desk.

The police left later that day, scratching their heads (although that may have been something to do with the headlice epidemic we had at St Egbert's that week). Everyone turned to me.

At first, I was fairly confident that I'd come up with an explanation for the theft, and be able to catch the culprit. But as the days wore on, everyone started looking grumpier and grumpier at me, and I started going redder and redder in the face. By the time the lice had been beaten back with sprays and lotions, I had to admit that I was beaten too.

Like I said, it was very embarrassing. Even more embarrassing than the time I wore my tattiest pants instead of my swimming trunks by mistake. And *that*

was oh-help-I-want-to-crawl-under-a-stone time!

Late one afternoon, I was sitting in my garden shed – or my Crime Headquarters, as I prefer to call it. I was flopped in my Thinking Chair – the battered old leather armchair where I do all my flopping and thinking.

I gazed around me at my desk, at my files of case notes, and at the gardening and DIY stuff I'm forced to share the shed with. I took off my glasses and gave them a quick polish with my sleeve. I stared out of the shed's perspex window.

I was utterly clueless. This case had got me more baffled than . . . than . . . good grief, there wasn't even a simile to describe how baffled I was! There were no clues and I had no idea how to uncover more information.

I let out a deep sigh and flicked back through my notebook, just in case there was some tiny detail I'd missed, something that would unlock the mystery.

'Who am I fooling?' I muttered to myself. 'There's no way I'm going to find out who stole that money now.'

Suddenly, there was a thunderous knocking at the shed door. I almost fell off my Thinking Chair in fright.

'Who's that?' I cried.

The door swung open and Bob Thompson stood there, blocking out the daylight like a slab of concrete with a head stuck on top of it. I shrank back a little in my Thinking Chair.

'H-hi, Bob,' I stuttered.

Bob Thompson was St Egbert's School's number one thug. In terms of sheer villainy, he was second only to my arch enemy, that low-down rat Harry Lovecraft. As readers of my earlier case files will know, Harry Lovecraft hatched his evil schemes using sneakiness, cunning, deceit and trickery. Bob Thompson just hit people. Everyone was scared of Bob Thompson. As he stood there, looming over me, three feeble thoughts kept running up and down in panic inside my head:

1. Oh dear, Bob Thompson knows where I live.
2. Oh dear, Bob Thompson's in my shed.
3. Oh dear, Bob Thompson's going to hit me.

'Please don't hit me,' I said.

Suddenly, he looked a little sheepish. 'Why would I do that?'

I sat up. 'Well, you hit most people,' I grumbled.

Now he looked sheepish enough to fool a shepherd. 'Yes, well, I suppose that's what I've come to talk to you about,' he said quietly.

I would have offered him my Thinking Chair to sit in, or my desk to perch on, but I had a feeling that neither of them would take the weight.

'How can I help you?' I said.

'Well, y'see,' he said. 'It was *me* who took that money from the office.'

Chapter Two

For a moment or two, I wasn't sure whether to be either a) relieved that the mystery was solved, or b) annoyed that I hadn't been able to track Bob down as the thief. Bob Thompson wasn't someone I'd ever have expected to outwit me. Out-thump me, yes, but not outwit me.

'How did you manage it?' I gasped. 'I take it you devised some brilliantly complex plot? You worked out a fiendishly clever method for pinpointing the cash and smuggling it out of the building?'

'No, I just snatched the money 'n' legged it.'

'Oh . . . But where did you go? Mrs McEwan came out of her office only a few seconds later and there was nobody around.'

'I hid behind the display boards in the waiting area,'

said Bob. 'There was a load of project work on Victorians pinned up there for visitors to look at.'

I slapped myself on the forehead. 'Of *course*!' I'd used exactly the same hiding place myself, during the case of *The Tomb of Death*. 'So you hadn't pre-planned the robbery at all?'

'No.'

I cleared my throat. 'Yes, well, it must have been the, umm, chance factor which threw me off the scent. Yes, that must be it.'

'I had to go to the office to give them a form,' said Bob. 'Just by chance there was nobody else in the corridor. Just by chance, Mrs McEwan turned away as I got to the office door. While she was giving her printer a good thump, I saw the money, and I took it. I hid behind the display boards until she went back into her office, then I legged it. I didn't know there'd be nobody about. I didn't even know that money would be sitting there on the desk. I just saw it there, and grabbed it. You do believe me, don't you?'

I had one good reason to believe him. There was a detail in his story which convinced me he was telling the truth.

Have you spotted it?

Mrs McEwan had asked me to keep quiet about having to give that very expensive printer of hers a good thump, to get it to work. If Bob knew about that too, he must have been there to witness it.

'Yes,' I said. 'I believe you. But why tell *me*? If you feel a sudden need to admit what you've done, why not go to the headteacher?'

'Because I can't return the money,' said Bob.

'Why not?'

'Because I haven't got it any more. I need your help to get it back.'

I sat back in my Thinking Chair, letting out a sarcastic blow of the lips which can't quite be put into words, but which was a sort of 'prrrrrrrp'. 'Let me get this straight. *You* steal some money, but you want *me* to sort things out for you?' I would have added 'I don't think so, matey,' but I reckoned there might still be a chance of getting thumped.

'No, it's not like that,' said Bob. He shuffled across the shed and sat droopily on my desk. It managed to take the weight OK after all. 'If I go to the Head without the money, then I'll just get into a lot of trouble. But if I can bring the money back, then that'll prove I've changed.'

'Changed?' I said.

Bob shifted from side to side. This might have been

because he was having difficulty saying what he wanted to say, or it might have been because he was sitting on a couple of pencils.

'Nicking that money has made me realise how . . . well, how nasty I've been to people all these years. What a bully I've been.'

I eyed him narrowly. 'How so?'

'I didn't nick that money just for myself,' said Bob quietly. 'I live in Herbert Street, near that row of shops on the corner. There's a gang of kids who hang out by those shops at night. They have a laugh, get into all sorts of bother, stuff like that, so I wanted to join them. But they've got this test you have to do before they'll let you be one of the gang. An initiation test. You have to steal something. Not just a packet of crisps from the newsagent's, something that's really worth something. Anyway, I saw that money and I thought it'd be the perfect thing to get me into the gang.'

'So you gave it to them?' I said.

Bob nodded. 'They were supposed to share it out, but they just laughed. They gave me a slap and told me to get lost.'

'What, *you*?'

'Most of them are even bigger than I am. They pushed me over, trod on me, sent me packing. I'd never had that happen to me before. I limped home. It made me think. I've been treating people like that for years, but now I've realised how they must have felt. I want to make amends. I want to, er, whassitcalled . . . turn over a new leaf.'

'And giving all the money back will show everyone you mean what you say,' I said.

'Right,' said Bob. 'If I can't give the money back, then it doesn't matter how much I say I've changed, nobody will believe me.'

'Hmm, you're right,' I said. 'OK, I'll help you. But only because it will make the playground a safer place! I'm doing this to stop half the school being frightened of you, it's not just for your benefit.'

He grinned at me with relief. Somehow, that was even more nerve-racking than having him loom menacingly over me.

'What else can you tell me?' I said. 'How do you know this gang haven't just spent the cash on . . . I dunno, whatever it is street gangs spend money on. Flowers for their mums, or something.'

'They always keep stolen stuff hidden for a while, until they're sure it's not being looked for any more,' said Bob. 'They put it somewhere away from where any of them live, so that if the police start sniffing around, they're not caught with it.'

'And where have they got this money stashed?'

'I don't know,' said Bob. 'Not exactly. All I can tell you is that it's hidden somewhere inside The Hangman's Lair.'

Chapter Three

THE HANGMAN'S LAIR WAS THE creepiest place in town. It was an area of woodland, about half a kilometre square, which stood between the back of a long, disjointed row of houses and the gently curving line of the local canal.

There had recently been talk of turning the place into a wildlife sanctuary, but nothing had ever come of it. I can't say I was surprised. There wasn't much wildlife living there. The place looked like it was meant for alligators or giant poisonous insects, but the most dangerous animal you ever saw around there was the occasional grumpy squirrel. The Hangman's Lair was somewhere the local wildlife tended to leave well alone.

It was so called because, legend had it, it was where

the town gallows had stood hundreds of years ago. And where, it was said, the town's mad, one-eyed hangman had lived in a tiny shack.

As soon as I entered the wood, the bright daylight was reduced to a shifting, colourless gloom. It was barely half an hour since school had finished for the day, but in The Hangman's Lair it could have been almost any time, or any season. I was surrounded by a dark criss-cross of claw-like branches. The trees, their trunks all ridged and cracked with age, grew in horrible twists which made them look as if they were straining and struggling to crawl up out of the ground. Under my school shoes was a patchwork of mud and leaves. Some fallen twigs and branches formed a hazy straight line which vanished among the tree trunks. The whole place was eerily quiet. Nothing seemed to move anywhere, and there was a smell of decay drifting through the damp air.

I looked around, hardly daring to move or make a sound. The woods didn't vary from one end to the other. Whatever direction you looked in, everything appeared almost exactly the same: trees and branches, as far as the eye could see. And the eye couldn't see all that far with all those trees and branches in the way. Standing there, I immediately understood why The Hangman's Lair had gained its reputation.

I took a slow, deep breath.

'Why didn't I bring anyone with me?' I muttered to myself. My words vanished on the air, absorbed by the earth and the canopy of twigs.

I could also understand why the gang from Herbert Street had chosen this spot to hide their loot in. Nobody would ever think of taking a pleasant stroll through The Hangman's Lair of an evening! Well, vampires and werewolves, possibly, but nobody else.

I looked left, right, up, down. That stolen money was hidden away in here somewhere, but *where*? Each tree looked like every other tree, and each patch of ground looked like every other patch of ground. You'd almost have to *live* in this horrible place to even find your way around. And so, unless I literally mapped out the entire . . .

Wait! Maybe the gang had made a map? Maybe there was no way to locate the money without it?

No. On second thoughts, definitely not. Bob told me that the gang hid stuff in case the police came 'sniffing around', as he put it. If the police came across a map pinpointing the location of the money, then the gang might as well not have hidden it in the first place. A location map would be ideal evidence.

Besides, this was a street gang we were talking about. Were they the sort of people who'd go to the time and trouble of making a map anyway? Well, they might when there was four hundred and twenty pounds at stake. Hmm, still seemed unlikely.

No, there was no map. Which meant that there was only one possibility left, as far as I could see. There *was* a way I could locate the money.

Have you worked it out?

The gang must have marked the hiding place somehow. Without a map, there'd be no other way of making sure they didn't lose track of the money.

Obviously, I wasn't going to find an 'X' carved into a tree trunk, or anything as blindingly obvious as that. But there had to be a mark of some kind. There had to be something, either on a tree, or marked on the ground, that would be distinctive enough to lead the gang back to the hiding place.

Actually, you know, thinking about it, the mark *could* be something obvious. The gang would hardly expect someone else, someone like me, to come looking for it. They *might* have left a mark in plain sight!

Two hours later, I came to the conclusion that they hadn't. Not only was there no mark in plain sight, there was no mark that I could 'sight' at all!

I'd combed The Hangman's Lair from end to end. I'd examined every tree, I'd squelched through every muddy puddle, I'd snagged my school uniform on every spiky twig. Nothing. No scratches in tree bark, no carefully placed piles of stones, no items tied to branches. There was nothing whatsoever that might have been a marker, a flag or a signpost. However they'd hidden that money, they'd hidden it very well.

By now, it was six p.m. It was starting to get dark, and the shadows beneath the trees were precisely deep enough to conceal everything from the outside world. You'd need to know exactly where you were going to find anything at that time, so further searching was pointless. Also, I was starting to get hungry. Also, I was starting to get quite scared, but I tried not to think about that.

On my way home, an unpleasant and worrying train of thought rumbled slowly through my mind, like an old-fashioned steam train chugging through a long, dark tunnel. By the time I turned the corner into my street, rapidly scribbling notes in my notebook, I'd come to a decision. I had a definite plan of action. And it wasn't one I was looking forward to.

I phoned my great friend Isobel 'Izzy' Moustique, St Egbert's School's all-round genius and official Princess of Facts and Figures. I needed to ask a couple of favours.

'First,' I said, 'see what you can find out about a gang of kids who hang around in Herbert Street. You know loads of people, someone will have come across them.'

'Okey-dokey,' she said. 'What's the case you're investigating this time?'

'Let's just say that if this works out, we'll be going on that school trip after all.'

'Great! I thought you'd drawn a total blank on the missing money,' she cried. 'You've finally got a lead?'

'Er, something like that,' I said hurriedly. 'Second, I need you to start a rumour.'

'A rumour? Why? What about?'

That plan of action I mentioned needed . . . hmm, what would you call it? It needed a certain amount of back-up. If my plan was going to work, there was some very specific information that had to be out there on the local grapevine.

See if you can spot what that information was, when it crops up in Chapter Four . . .

A Page From My Notebook

My train of thought:

1. That money is so well hidden that I'd need a lot of time to find it, and probably some help too.
2. I can't afford to delay. For one thing, the gang might retrieve the money and spend it. (And for another thing, the school trip that four hundred and twenty pounds was for is supposed to take place in a couple of weeks!)
3. I can't afford to get help searching. Too much risk of being spotted, and the gang being alerted to what's going on.
4. If I can't SEARCH for the money, there's only one alternative . . .

My plan of action:

1. Make contact with the gang. They don't know me, and I don't know them. This is a vital advantage.
2. Convince them . . . somehow . . . that I have something they want. Something worth four hundred and twenty pounds. (Note to self: Yes, but WHAT?? Must think of something!)
3. Secretly follow them . . . somehow . . . when they retrieve the money from The Hangman's Lair.

4. Persuade them . . . somehow . . . to hand over the cash BEFORE I give them this whatever-it-is I haven't thought of yet.
5. Run for it.

Problem A: Not at all sure about point 5. Should rethink that bit.
Problem B: My plan of action has potential pitfalls and dangers all over it! I am NOT looking forward to this.

Chapter Four

THE NEXT DAY, I WAS in the dinner queue at school when something made me almost jump out of my skin. The sight of a school dinner can sometimes do that. Or the sight of a school dinner lady. However, in this case, I almost jumped out of my skin because I heard a loud 'Pssst!' behind me. I turned round and found myself face-to-shoulder with Bob Thompson.

'How's it going?' he whispered.

'Oh, er, fine, y'know, er, making progress,' I said.

'Is there anything I can do to help?'

'I have a plan of action worked out, but it relies on the Herbert Street gang not knowing who I am, or that you have any connection with me. If they get wind that you're involved, they'd smell something fishier than a plate of fish fingers in fish sauce with extra fish on top. So, thanks, but no.'

'Oi, are you having yer dinner or what?' squarked a dinner lady at me. I almost jumped out of my skin again. As Bob lumbered away, a dollop of today's delicious, nutritious recipe was slopped down in front of me. It appeared to be fish fingers in fish sauce with extra fish on top.

'Yummy,' I said, with a painted-on grin.

I spotted Izzy and hurried over to sit next to her. She had a book open on the table in front of her.

'Hi,' I said. My eyes did a quick zip around the room to check that nobody could overhear me. It made me feel slightly giddy, and I made a mental note not to do that again. 'Have you managed to set that rumour going?'

'Yes,' said Izzy. 'I talked loudly in front of a couple of serious gossips, and I posted stuff on the forums of a couple of websites.'

'Excellent. Give it a day or so for the news to get around, and then I can put Operation Hangman's Lair into, er, operation. Anyway, later on I'll —'

'Listen,' hissed Izzy. 'This morning I've also asked around about these Herbert Street kids. I think you should pack this whole scheme in. Now.'

'Why?' I said.

'At the school they go to, on the other side of town,

they have the worst reputation you can possibly imagine. They're bullies on a level which makes Bob Thompson look like a great big softie who cries a lot!'

'Yes, I realise they're not exactly nice.'

'"Not exactly nice?"' spluttered Izzy. 'They've all been in trouble with the police, two of them for breaking into cars. One of them has a scar on his face that he got in a fight, and another's got four older brothers who are all in prison for armed robbery!'

'I've promised I'll get that money back, and that's what I'll do,' I said. 'I've never given up on a case yet, and I never will.'

'That's all very well,' said Izzy, 'but if this scheme of yours doesn't work, they are going to be *after* you, Saxby. And when they catch you, they're not just going to ruffle your hair a bit.'

'Ooh, I hate it when someone does that,' I muttered.

'Quite. I mean, no offence, but you're not exactly the sporty type, are you? You're not very tall, you've mended your glasses with a plaster, and your idea of strenuous exercise is getting up in the morning.'

'OK, I know I'm a bit . . . geeky . . . but —'

'But nothing. If *anything* goes wrong, they are going to *flatten* you, do you understand that?'

'Of course I do,' I said bravely.

I didn't *feel* brave. I felt very, very nervous. Izzy was

right. I couldn't allow one single thing to go wrong with my plan of action. And I still hadn't quite worked out what some of it was going to be!

Later that day, I went to see my other great friend George 'Muddy' Whitehouse, the school's King of Gadgets and Fixer of All Mechanical Things. I wondered if, possibly, maybe, he might be able to help me out, perhaps, perchance, on the next stage of Operation Hangman's Lair, the following afternoon.

'Undercover work?' he cried. 'You bet! Fantastic!'

'Just let me do all the talking, OK? You only need to be there to agree with what I'm saying.'

'Should I wear a disguise?'

'What, dark glasses and a false beard? No, I don't think your usual approach to disguises would be quite right. Your normal look will be fine: scruffy, covered in mud and food stains. Anything except school uniform. We don't want to give them too many clues as to who we really are, just in case.'

'Just in case what?' asked Muddy.

'So, anyway, tomorrow after school, let's meet up at quarter to four. See you . . .'

We entered Herbert Street at precisely 4:22 p.m. the following afternoon. I judged that enough time had now elapsed to allow Izzy's deliberately-started rumour to spread through the non-adult community. I hoped my judgement was right: if the rumour hadn't spread far enough, I was going to have a very tough time fooling the gang with the pack of lies I was about to tell.

'Is that a fake moustache?' I whispered angrily.

'Only a little one,' mumbled Muddy, covering his top lip. 'I figured that if these kids are older than us, it might help if —'

'Take it off! Now!'

Muddy peeled the hairy thing away from under his nose and stuffed it into his pocket which was, as usual, full to bursting point with assorted gizmos and broken odds and ends.

'Remember,' I whispered. 'Let me do the talking.'

Herbert Street was a wide road, with a huge traffic roundabout at one end and a small, weed-strewn children's play area at the other. The road surface was a patchwork of greys, where it had been dug up over and over again, and the broad pavements were busy with cracked paving slabs and shreds of wind-blown litter. The houses on each side of the road were modern and boxy, with identical wooden canopies above the front doors, and chain-link fences fixed to concrete posts.

I wondered for a moment which house Bob Thompson lived in. Probably the one with the broken fridge on the front lawn.

Towards the roundabout end of Herbert Street was a row of shops, fronted with a long, blank-looking run of parking bays. There was a newsagent's, a chip shop, a Chinese takeaway, a big shop that sold spare parts for cars and a laundrette with *Wash-O-Mat* across the window in faded letters.

The area around the shops was surprisingly lively. People were coming and going in a regular, steady stream. Cars were crawling in and out of parking slots every couple of minutes.

There were several groups of kids in sight. A cluster of teenage girls scuttered past the newsagent's, tapping at their phones and telling each other things which appeared to be very, very important.

Muddy eyed them carefully. 'Is that the gang?'

I looked at him. 'Somehow, I don't think so.'

'Well, what do we look for?' he said. 'We can't go over there and shout, "Hands up anyone here who's nicked some money recently", can we?!'

There was an easy way to identify the Herbert Street gang. Something Izzy had said would make at least one of them recognisable.

Do you remember what it was?

'That's them, over there,' I said. 'Izzy told me that one of them has a scar on his face. See the kid in the red coat?'

Five boys were perched on the bonnet of a chunky BMW, laughing and jostling each other. The one in the red coat had a livid groove in his skin, which ran from the bridge of his nose, round his cheek to his chin. And he was the least scary-looking of them. They all had hair which was close-cropped into a tangle of points, like a wild lawn. Their faces were angular and flecked with acne.

A man in blue overalls suddenly came hurrying out of the car spares shop. He shouted at the gang to gerrof his car, go-ooon, gerrof with yer! They jeered at him as they slid along the bonnet of the BMW and dropped to the ground. Once the man had hurried inside again, they regrouped on the bonnet of the next car along, like pigeons scattering and then returning to their territory.

'Don't forget . . .' I said.

'Let you do the talking.'

'Right. You set?'

'Yup. You?'

'Yup. Ready?'

'Yup. You?'

'Yup. Right, let's go.'

'Go.'

'Go, yup, right.'

We walked as casually as our shaking legs would allow. I could feel my heart pattering as if it was trying to shove the rest of my innards aside and make a run for it before it was too late.

We approached the gang, trying to make sure we didn't even glance in their direction. This part of Operation Hangman's Lair needed us to lure the gang into talking to us first, not *us* talking to *them* first. As we got within earshot of them, I nudged Muddy and we sat down on the kerb.

'This is all your fault!' I said, loud enough for them to hear, but soft enough to make it appear that I didn't *mean* them to hear. 'If you hadn't got greedy and nicked the whole lot, we wouldn't be in this mess.'

'Hey, woooow, man; take a chill pill, bro,' said Muddy. Then he did a weird hand gesture he'd seen on a music video.

'What are you *doing*?' I whispered through clenched teeth.

'I'm getting into character. I'm being a street gang member.'

'You're being a complete twit!' I whispered. 'Act natural.'

I heard movement behind us. Shoes crunching against the pavement. My heart started making a bid for freedom again.

'I did what you wanted,' I said, loud-but-not-obviously-loud. 'I distracted the sales guy. If you'd snatched half a dozen, he'd never have spotted what we'd done. But no, you have to bundle a whole drawerful into your school bag. Now we've got the cops after us.'

There was a long pause. Cars growled past. A breeze fluttered litter into the road.

'Oi!' called someone behind us.

Bingo.

We turned. All five of the gang were standing a couple of metres away. The one with the scar had pulled the hood of his coat up. Another of them, the tallest, took a step closer. I got the impression he was their unofficial leader. His head was so rectangular I half expected to have seen it in a maths lesson somewhere. His eyes were piggy and kind of squashed together, as if someone had got hold of his ears and pulled all his features forwards.

'Who're you?' he grunted.

'Ask 'em why the cops are after them, Moz,' said the one with the scar.

'Shut up, Zippy, I'll ask 'em what I want,' said Moz.

'Don't call me Zippy,' muttered Zippy.

Moz sniffed noisily at us. 'Why the cops after you, then?'

'Oh no, they heard you!' cried Muddy suddenly. 'It's

all over! We're found out! We're rumbled! We're going to get got by the cops! Oh, you mad fool! They overheard everything you —'

I interrupted him with a stare which could have turned milk sour.

'It's nothing, really,' I said to Moz. 'We'll be going now, nice to meet you n'all.'

I half-turned to leave, but Moz jabbed me on the shoulder and half-turned me back. 'I said, why are the cops after you? We don't want police coming round here. What's your name?'

'I'm . . . Steve,' I said. 'And this is —'

'Bond,' piped up Muddy. 'James Bond. Like the spy. It's a bit embarrassing him having the same name as me, actually. But, y'know, it impresses the girls, and when I —'

I interrupted him with a stare which could have knocked a charging rhino on its back.

'That a code name is it?' grinned Moz. 'You doing undercover work?'

My blood turned to ice. The rest of the gang sniggered.

'Don't pay any attention to him,' I said, 'he has to have a teaching assistant all to himself at school.'

'Give 'em a slap, Moz,' said Zippy.

'Belt up, Zippy, I'll slap who I like,' said Moz. 'You

two looking for a slap? I want to know why the cops are after you.'

'It's his fault,' I said, nodding at Muddy. 'We went into Gamebusters the other day. We were going to steal that new one, *Maximum Death IV*. So I distracted the guy behind the till, I pulled a display over and made out I was hurt. He comes out from behind the counter, and Mr Brilliant here is supposed to nip round to the big drawers, find the right disc, stick a few in his pocket and run.'

Moz eyed us. 'But . . .?'

'But my friend here decides to take the lot and dump them into his school bag. One hundred and forty games. Then we're out the door before the shop assistant knows what's happening.'

'I don't know what came over me!' cried Muddy. 'I went funny in the brain! Greed overtook my mind! I was mad for games and more games! The red mists descended and —'

I interrupted him with a stare which could have melted concrete.

'And now you think the police are going to come banging on your door?' said Moz.

'We've *never* stolen anything before, *ever*,' I said. 'And we never will again. Instead of harmlessly killing zombies, we've got a huge pile of nicked gear to worry about! We only wanted to nick *Maximum Death IV* because we had no money, and it's rated adults-only, so the shop wouldn't have sold it to us anyway, even if we *did* have the money.'

'When was this?' said Moz, suspiciously.

'A couple of days ago,' I said.

'Hey, Moz,' said Zippy, suddenly. 'I think I heard about that. My sister said she'd heard something about two kids who snatched a load of computer games.'

'Yeah, I heard that too,' said one of the others. 'My mate's girlfriend said.'

'Looks like you two are going to be front page news around here,' smiled Moz.

'Oh no!' I cried. (You know, I ought to give acting a go. I had just the right note of fear and panic in my voice). 'This is awful. We're not crooks. We just did a very bad thing, just the once. Come on . . . James . . . we're going to go and throw all those discs away. Get rid of them.'

'Hang on,' said Zippy. 'Don't chuck 'em. I know someone with a market stall. You could make a load of money.'

'Button yer lip, Zippy,' said Moz. 'I'll say if they get chucked or not.' He looked down at me with those squashed-up eyes of his. 'Yeah, don't chuck 'em, Steve, you could make a load of money.'

'No,' I said. 'No, no, no, no way. That'd make things even worse. No, those discs are getting binned. Right now.'

Come on, Moz, I thought to myself, think the thought I want you to think! There's a great idea just sitting there, waiting for you to find it! My heart was racing and my legs were starting to get shaky.

Zippy leaned over and whispered to Moz. Moz stared at him for a second or two, then turned back to me and Muddy.

'I've had a great idea,' said Moz. 'If you don't want to make a load of money, then we will. You can give *us* those discs.'

'No,' I said, 'I don't want to risk walking around with them. The cops might pick us up!'

'Don't talk rubbish,' sneered Moz. 'You fetch those discs, now, and you give them to us, or you get a pounding. Understand?'

I hadn't reckoned on this. Foolishly, I'd assumed that they would offer to buy the discs off us. I'd underestimated them. My stomach rolled over in slow motion. I now had to take a risk.

'We'll sell them to you,' I said.

Moz loomed forward. He stood with the toes of his trainers almost touching my shoes. He jabbed a grubby finger against my chest. 'I hope you like hospital food,

Steve, 'cos if you don't do what I tell you, you'll be having a lot of it.'

I stood absolutely still. Which wasn't easy, when my legs felt like they were shouting 'Run away!' and the rest of me felt like it was agreeing with my legs.

'You can have the discs,' I said, in as un-wobbly a voice as I could manage. 'But we want paying for them.'

'If you don't give me those discs,' growled Moz, 'I'll set my gang on you.'

'If you set your gang on me,' I said, 'I wouldn't give you those discs in a million years. You know you can make a big profit. Pay up, and we all get something out of this. Otherwise, everyone loses. Your choice.'

I tried to steady my breathing. I couldn't let Moz think I'd back down. I had to convince him that I meant what I said. I glared up at him, hoping that my expression said 'I Mean Business', rather than 'I Want To Go Home'.

At last, Moz emitted a loud snort and turned to the rest of the gang. 'I like this kid. He reminds me of me.'

Eurgh, I thought to myself.

'How many games d'ya say you got?' said Moz.

'A hundred and forty,' I said.

He glanced around at the traffic, as if the next thing he was going to say could be seen painted on the side of a passing van. 'You'll take one pound for each.'

I shook my head quickly. 'No. Five is fair. You can sell them for three times that. You can triple your money, easy.'

'Two pounds each, no more than that,' said Moz.

'Four,' I said. 'Four, or forget it.'

'Three.'

I pretended to have a careful think about that. 'Three,' I said at last. 'Hundred and forty times three . . . That's . . . That's four hundred and twenty pounds, exactly . . . Hmm . . . OK, three for each. You've got that amount of money, have you?'

Moz snorted again. So did the rest of the gang. They were starting to sound like a herd of buffalo.

'Yeah, we've got plenty of money,' smiled Moz. 'Haven't we, lads?'

The rest of them laughed. Zippy giggled into his coat hood.

'OK,' I said. 'We'll meet right here, tomorrow morning, eight o'clock. I don't want to wait, I want to get rid of this gear as soon as I can.'

'Shut it, Steve,' said Moz, 'I say when we meet. Eight it is, then. If you're not here on time, you and your secret agent friend here are going to get a pounding. Understand?'

Without another word, Muddy and I hurried away. We were half a kilometre away from Herbert Street before either of us dared even breathe.

'Phew, that was close,' gasped Muddy.

'Which part of "Let me do the talking" was confusing you there?' I asked.

'We did it, didn't we?' said Muddy. 'We convinced them.'

'We certainly convinced them you're a complete twerp.'

'Which works in our favour,' said Muddy. 'If they think we're a couple of bumbling amateurs when it comes to crime, they won't suspect we're trying to pull the wool over their eyes.'

'Yes, I suppose so,' I said. 'But remember, if they discover we've just told them a pack of lies, and that there are no stolen discs, and that we really *are* working undercover . . . we're going to get a pounding.'

'Er, yeah, that bit I got,' said Muddy.

'Come on,' I said, 'we've got work to do!'

A Page From My Notebook

Operation Hangman's Lair: Status Report – at the mid-point in the plan, all is well so far. Just. Must now think carefully about final stages of the operation!

Beware! I'm sure the Herbert Street gang have NO INTENTION of giving us a penny. Right now, I reckon, they're planning to flash the cash at us tomorrow morning, then boot us aside the minute we've revealed where the discs are. I'm sure they'll be planning to get away with the discs, the money, the lot.

Sneaky! If the next bit goes according to plan, we won't have to worry about their double-crossing tactics.

Beware, part 2! However, the next bit is probably the riskiest of the lot. For this, we will need:

- 2 x Whitehouse Personal Communicators With Ear Attachments (as made by Muddy from a couple of old mobile phones)
- 2 pairs x Whitehouse Ultra-Soft Shoe Covers (as made by Muddy for creeping out of the house after being grounded)
- 6 x Whitehouse Dazzletron 6000 Mega-Beam Lamps (as made by Muddy from a load of car headlights)
- 1 x Whitehouse Sound Amplifier And Distorter (as made by Muddy to scare the poo out of the hideous little brats next door).

CHAPTER FIVE

A LITTLE WHILE LATER, MUDDY and I were hiding behind a hedge on Deadman's Lane, close to the edge of The Hangman's Lair. Beside us was Muddy's tatty old school bag, bulging with the equipment I'd listed in my notebook.

'Don't you ever clean that bag?' I whispered, peering at it snootily and wrinkling up my nose.

'I think it's only the mud stains which hold it together,' whispered Muddy. 'Can't we hide on the other side of the road? I think my trousers are soaking something up.'

'No,' I said, 'we wait here. The gang should be along in about ten minutes.'

Muddy thought for a moment.

'How do you know they won't enter the wood from the other end, way over there?' he said.

'I don't *know*,' I replied, 'but it's likely they'll come past us here. Herbert Street is back in *that* direction, so unless they're going to go completely out of their way and circle around to the other end of the wood, then they'll be coming along here.'

Muddy thought for another moment.

'How can you possibly know what time they'll come to retrieve the money?'

'I don't *know*,' I replied, 'but I can make a good guess. We *do* know it'll have to be before tomorrow morning, of course, so they'll make their move tonight. They'll want to fetch the money when there's the least chance of them being spotted, a time when it's dark enough to be hidden in those woods, but light enough to find your way, if you know where you're going.'

Think back to my previous visit to The Hangman's Lair. There was a specific hour at which conditions in there would be exactly right for the gang to move around with minimal risk.

Did you make a note of the time?

'When I came here the other day,' I said to Muddy, 'it became too shadowy to search at six p.m., just when it was getting dark. My guess is that the Herbert Street gang will be here in precisely . . .' I checked my watch. '. . . four minutes.'

Six and a half minutes later, all five members of the gang came scuffing along Deadman's Lane. Moz walked in front, with Zippy just behind him, looking around in all directions.

'There you go,' I whispered with a grin. 'Only two and a half minutes out. Not bad.'

The gang made a sharp turn between two houses, heading for the woods. Muddy and I clipped the Whitehouse Personal Communicators to our ears, and slipped the Whitehouse Ultra-Soft Shoe Covers over our trainers.

'You're going to have to work on these communicators, Muddy,' I whispered, as we scuttled across the road, crouched down. 'My head keeps lolling over.'

'Yeah, the weight's a problem,' whispered Muddy. 'I had to use larger batteries than normal.'

'We look like we're wearing giant earrings,' I spluttered.

'At least if the gang spot us,' hissed Muddy, 'they'll be too busy laughing to give us a pounding.'

'Shh,' I hissed. 'They've stopped. Keep down.'

Moz had paused at the outer edge of the trees. For a couple of seconds, I was terrified that one of them had heard us. But then Moz and Zippy said something to each other that I couldn't overhear, and with one last glance over their shoulders, they all disappeared into The Hangman's Lair.

I beckoned to Muddy and we followed, keeping as low to the ground as we could. Those Whitehouse Ultra-Soft Shoe Covers did a perfect job of silencing our footsteps. However, silent footsteps seemed a bit pointless when the gear in Muddy's bag kept clanking around.

'Keep it steady,' I whispered.

'You carry it, then,' whispered Muddy crossly.

'Keep it steady,' I whispered. 'Come on, we can't let them get too far ahead, or we'll lose them in the shadows.'

Now that the gang were under the cover of the twisting, spiky branches, they were marching straight ahead and not bothering to keep a lookout behind them. The sounds of their crunching against fallen twigs was enough to mask any slight noises Muddy and I were making.

We darted from the shadow of one tree trunk to another. There had been heavy rain the night before, and the bark still felt damp and slippery. A smell of wet, sagging vegetation had been stirred up all through The Hangman's Lair.

With the gang well inside the wood, I was starting to wonder about the method they'd used to mark the place where they'd hidden the money. Before, you'll remember, I'd found no trace of anything that might lead me to the cash. Now, I was watching them carefully, eager to see what tiny little detail I might have missed.

'Here's the line,' said Moz. 'It's up this way.'

I risked going a few steps closer, to get a look at what he was talking about. On the ground, fallen twigs and branches formed a hazy straight line which vanished among the tree trunks, and which the gang were now following.

I almost gave myself a clunk on the head. I'd *seen* that line last time I was here (see page 16), but I hadn't realised what it meant! Had they simply marked a trail?

A minute or two later, the answer was clear. The gang stopped at a murky spot in front of a plain, anonymous-looking tree. On the ground, the straight line they'd been following came to an end, and where it ended it was joined by two other lines, one to each side of the original line, and vanishing off into the darkness at angles of around forty-five degrees.

No, they hadn't marked a trail. They'd placed the

shape of a gigantic arrow on the ground, pointing to the hiding place! Unless you knew the arrow was there, you'd never have spotted it. I'd been looking for something too small!

'Oh, that's clever,' I muttered, admiringly. 'You've got to admit, that's clever.'

'Shhh,' hissed Muddy. 'This is it.'

'Give me the shovel, Moz,' said Zippy, 'and I'll dig it up.'

'What shovel?' said Moz. 'You can see I'm not carrying any shovel! What do you think I've got, some sort of magical giant pocket or something?'

'What am I going to dig it up with?' said Zippy.

'That's your problem, mate,' grunted Moz.

The others laughed. I nudged Muddy.

'Now's our chance, while they're distracted,' I whispered. 'You take two of the lamps, I'll position the rest.'

Muddy nodded. I took the bag and crept away, moving in a wide semi-circle around the gang. Every few metres, I stopped and wedged one of the Whitehouse Dazzletron 6000 Mega-Beam Lamps into the tree branches beside me. When the last one was in place, I crouched down and waited, silently.

By now the gang had stopped arguing about shovels and had made Zippy unearth the money with his bare hands. He dropped to his knees and started digging with his fingers, grumbling and griping under his breath.

I watched from behind a mass of undergrowth, never taking my eyes off the spot where Zippy was digging. I was shaking with nerves, half of me thrilled by Operation Hangman's Lair, and the other half of me scared to death in case some fang-toothed woodland monster suddenly oozed up out of the ground at me.

Zippy sat back, slopping mud off his hands. 'There it is. Safe and sound.'

He reached into the hole he'd dug and pulled out a tightly wrapped bundle. It slurped against the earth, as if the woods were trying to hang on to it. By now, the sun had set and the shadows beneath the trees were thickening into the inky chill of night. I could barely make out the bundle in Zippy's hand. It was rolled into a plastic shopping bag and secured with brown parcel tape, to keep the moisture out.

'Now, Muddy,' I whispered into my communicator. 'Switch on now.'

Suddenly, six sharp white beams of light flashed into life. I blinked in the harsh glare. The gang were dazzled, screwing up their eyes and shielding themselves with their hands. Everything was suddenly lit up, every tiny detail of the woods standing out, bright and stark against the blackness beyond.

'What the —' yelled Moz.

Quickly, I raised the Whitehouse Sound Amplifier And Distorter to my lips. Thanks to Muddy's skill with all things electronic, my voice emerged sounding very deep, very angry and very loud. 'This is the police! You are surrounded! Raise your hands and stand still! We've caught the kids who stole those computer games, and now we've caught you!'

For the tiniest split fraction of a micro-second, the gang stood there, faces bleached by the light beams, eyes goggling, jaws dangling like kiddies' swings in a gale. Then Moz yelled, 'Leg it!'

Like crows startled off a fence, they flapped into motion with an almighty series of squawks. Zippy dropped the bundle of money with a yelp and bounded away into the dark, pushing the others aside.

'Halt!' boomed my distorted voice. 'Stay where you are! Get 'em, Sergeant! Arrest those youths! Oi! Come back 'ere!'

We gave them time to get clear of The Hangman's Lair, then Muddy switched the lamps off. By now, we'd both started giggling, but the sudden darkness that fell on us when the lights went out quickly shut us up.

I picked up the bundle, stumbling slightly in the gloom. I pulled a small tear in one end of it, and there, inside, was a wad of crumpled banknotes.

'Mission accomplished,' I whispered with a smile.

'Come on, let's get out of this creepy place,' said Muddy.

Chapter Six

AT PRECISELY 8:22 A.M. THE following morning, I walked past the school gates with more spring in my step than a pair of rocket-powered ejector-boots. I couldn't quite decide whether to whistle a happy tune or adopt a mile-wide grin, so I must have looked as though my mouth was trying to dance a tango. But I didn't much care. The four hundred and twenty pounds was tucked into my pocket. I'd counted the money when I got home from The Hangman's Lair, and I'd resealed the bundle. It was all there, safe and sound.

Muddy was sitting on the low wall outside the main school building, reading his dog-eared copy of this month's *Engineering Projects Round-Up*. As soon as he spotted me, he stuffed the magazine into his bag and dashed over to me, his shoelaces flapping around his ankles.

'We did it!' he said, almost jumping up and down with excitement.

'With a bit of luck,' I said, 'the gang will be in hiding for a few weeks. And even if they turned up to our pre-arranged meeting, let's see . . . about twenty minutes ago, the fact that we're not there should confirm the idea that the police have caught up with us.'

'Hah! You think of everything!' cried Muddy.

I pulled the taped-up plastic bag out of my bag. 'Yes,' I said quietly. 'I do. I must say, I'm relieved that this case has come to a successful conclusion. A couple of weeks ago, I was worried that my skills as a brilliant schoolboy detective were going down the pan. But now, once again, I can say that nobody gets the better of Saxby Smart.'

'Too right!' declared Muddy. 'Look, there's Bob Thompson. Shall we give him the good news?'

'Let's,' I said.

Bob Thompson was lumbering past the gates, a worried expression on his face. As he looked up, I beckoned him over and he veered across the flow of kids like a huge cruise ship changing course.

'H-have you got it?' he asked nervously.

I held up the taped bundle. 'Safe and sound,' I said.

His face melted into joy. 'Thank you! I've been so

worried the past few days. You don't know what this means to me. I really owe you one. Now I can take the money back to the office, and put everything right, and start turning over that new leaf at last.'

'Are you sure you don't want me to return it to the head?' I said. 'I'd happily tell her the full story.'

'No,' said Bob, 'I must do it myself. I must admit what I did, it's important.'

'Y'know,' said Muddy, 'I never thought I'd hear myself say this, but I admire your guts, Bob.'

'Thanks,' said Bob with a feeble smile.

I handed Bob the bundle.

His feeble smile suddenly became rather more confident. Then, with one lumbering movement, he barged Muddy and me over. We thudded painfully on to the tarmac.

'Suckers!' he brayed loudly. 'What a couple of prize dipsticks!'

Muddy almost exploded with rage. 'You liar! You double-crossing, back-stabbing, no-good, miserable . . .' And the rest of that sentence I can't repeat here.

With a snort of triumph, Bob Thompson turned and trotted off. He growled at other kids to get out of his way. They did as they were told.

'We're not going to let him get away with that!' cried Muddy. 'Are we?'

'No, we certainly are not,' I said. 'Come on, he's heading back out of the gates. We're going to follow him.'

We had to hurry, to keep up with the pace of his tree-trunk-leg strides. He walked out of the school, crossed the road and turned left towards the town centre. Muddy and I trailed along at a distance, keeping hidden around corners and behind bus stops wherever we could. All the way, Muddy kept muttering more sentences I can't repeat here.

After a few minutes, it was clear where Bob Thompson was heading. Herbert Street.

'I don't get it,' said Muddy. 'Is he going back to the gang? He's not going to return the money to them, surely?'

'Looks like it,' I said. I was already getting out of breath. (Yeah, yeah, I know, Izzy was right, I need to get more exercise, nag, nag, but I never seem to have the time, blah, blah, blah.)

'Why would he do that?' said Muddy.

'Remember how he told me that he wanted to join the Herbert Street gang?' I gasped.

'Yes.'

'And remember how there was an initiation test, a test he had to pass before they'd let him join?'

'Yes.'

'Well, something occurs to me. I don't think stealing the money was the initiation test. I think that was only part of it. I think the real test was to *get it back* from where the gang hid it.'

'You mean, he's used us to do his dirty work for him?' said Muddy. 'He didn't have the brains to pass the test and work out how to find it and nick it back from the gang, so he came to *you*?'

'Exactly,' I said.

'That nasty, gutter-dragging . . .' Muddy went back to muttering sentences I can't repeat here.

A couple of minutes later, Bob Thompson turned the corner into Herbert Street. Muddy and I managed to shadow him all the way to the row of shops, by keeping low behind the dotted line of parked cars on the opposite side of the road.

We peeked out from behind a battered-looking blue van. We were just in time to see Bob approach the gang. As before, they were slumped around the nearest car. So much for them being in hiding for a few weeks, I thought to myself.

We were too far away to hear what was being said, but we caught a general tone of friendly greeting as Bob walked up to Moz. As soon as Bob produced the bundle, the gang all sat up, looked at each other and started laughing. Bob launched into an explanation.

'He'll be going on about how cleverly he's tricked them,' I said quietly.

'It's not fair,' groaned Muddy. 'Someone *has* got the better of you, after all! A rotten bully like Bob Thompson, too!'

The gang were thoroughly enjoying Bob's story. They kept shaking their heads and pulling dopey faces. I could imagine what they were saying – 'So *you* put those kids up to it, man? Yeah? Aww, that was genius! We totally fell for it, didn't we? Duh! Didn't spot that one coming, man, we expected you to ambush one of us and start thumping until you got given the location!'

Moz, cackling loudly, batted Bob on the shoulder. Bob flipped the bundle into the air for Moz to catch, and as it dropped into Moz's hands the rest of the gang began to cheer and clap. Moz ripped open the end of the bundle, and pulled out the contents.

A handful of newspaper, cut to the size of banknotes.

'Is this a *joke*?' roared Moz. Ah, now *that* we could hear. 'Where's our *money*?'

Bob said something in a high-pitched whine. He started flapping his hands about. He grabbed the bundle back and tore it apart. No money.

'Give me that money!' shouted Moz. 'Or you get a pounding! Right now!'

Slowly, Muddy turned his head to face me.

'Saxbyyyyy?' he said.

'I told you I think of everything,' I smiled. 'I swapped it over last night.'

A furious row had erupted over the road. Bob and Moz were yelling into each other's faces, Zippy was shouting at the pair of them, and the rest of the gang were circling like vultures around a dead wildebeest.

Soon, the shouting became pushing and the pushing became raised fists. Seconds later, Bob was making a run for it, pursued by the gang who were bellowing for revenge.

'Come on,' I said to Muddy. 'We'd better hurry if we're going to make it back to school before the bell goes.'

We scurried back the way we'd come.

'How did you know he was going to double-cross us like that?' said Muddy.

'Weeelll,' I said, 'I didn't *know*, but I had a definite suspicion. You see, I could believe his whole story, except for one little detail.'

'Which was . . .?'

Have you spotted it?

'He said the gang had taken the cash and sent him packing. Something about that didn't seem quite right. Bullies like Bob Thompson don't back off that easily. Besides, if it had happened exactly as he claimed, how did he know that the gang had later buried the money in The Hangman's Lair? He must have seen them go in there.'

'So you suspected him all along?' said Muddy.

'A bit,' I said. 'I suppose I *wanted* to believe him. After all, the prospect of one less bully is always welcome. But, as it turned out, I was right. What he told me was a pack of lies from the start.'

'And your reputation as a brilliant schoolboy detective remains intact!' said Muddy.

'Ahhh, yeeeeah, there is that too,' I said.

We just had time before Registration to return the money to the school office. Once the Head had stopped thanking me and counted the cash for the umpteenth time, she asked me how I'd managed to track it down.

I thought for a moment, then asked her if that info could remain confidential. I told her that the person who'd stolen the money was receiving, er, punishment for what he'd done, that justice had been served, and that perhaps in this instance the matter was best left alone. She was clearly reluctant to agree, but in the end her happiness at having the money back won the day.

That afternoon, I returned home and went straight to my garden shed. I plonked myself down in my Thinking Chair, propped my feet up on my desk and added some notes to my files.

Case closed.

Case File Eleven:

Diary of Fear

Chapter One

'Hmm,' I said to myself.

I scratched my chin and looked around me. 'Hmm,' I said to myself again.

I hadn't the faintest idea what to do now. So I just said, 'Hmm,' again.

I was standing in the middle of the small back garden behind my house. I was in the middle of the lawn and in the middle of a random pile of boxes, paint tins, the lawnmower, a coil of hose, toolboxes, my desk, my filing cabinet of case notes and my Thinking Chair.

I was having a tidy-out of the shed. And it wasn't going well. There must be a way to get a bit more space in here, I'd thought to myself. There must be some way to arrange all these tonnes of *stuff* so that I'm not having to squeeze around everything all the time.

So I'd emptied the whole lot out on to the lawn. But now, standing there, staring at it all, I hadn't the faintest idea where to begin. It wouldn't have been so bad if I hadn't been forced to share my shed with all that gardening and DIY gear, but there was nowhere else for it to go.

'Hmm,' I said, as if saying it enough times and looking thoughtful would somehow give me the answer. I was sure there was more stuff here than I'd started with . . .

'Hello?' came a voice from the other side of the garden gate. I looked up to see Amy Parsons, a girl from school.

Everyone called her Parsnip, which they told her was because of her name, but which was actually because she had a nose like a parsnip. She had her long black hair tied up in a tight bun, and was wearing a pair of high-fashion jeans and a purple longsleeved T-shirt, thick with dust at the knees and elbows. Multi-coloured stripey socks poked up from the tops of her almost-new, polished shoes. Her pockets were clearly full of various odds and ends and, as she pulled a stray strand of hair back into place behind her ear, I noticed that the ends of her fingers were grubby. Her face showed a mixture of worry and weariness.

'Have I come at the wrong time?' she said, looking at the heaps that were littering the lawn.

'No,' I said, 'you've come at exactly the right time. I'm looking for an excuse to leave all this where it is and ignore it for as long as possible. Here, have my Thinking Chair. I haven't got any other actual seats.'

She perched on the battered old armchair. It seemed very weird seeing it sitting there in the open air. Out in broad daylight, it looked even more saggy and worn-out than it did in the shed. I pulled up a couple of half empty paint tins and sat on those. They were extremely uncomfortable.

'I need your help,' said Amy. 'But I don't know where to begin.'

'Well,' I shrugged, 'a certain amount is clear to me already. You've recently lost a personal item, a small one. After an extensive search, you have – in the last couple of hours – come to the conclusion that it has been stolen. It's probably not something that's valuable in terms of money, but it's very precious to you. You also need to get it back urgently.'

She stared at me for a moment, boggle-eyed.

'Yes,' she said at last, 'that's right. All of it. How could you *possibly* know all that?'

'From your appearance,' I said.

There was one detail about her in particular that had given me my first clue. And everything else could be deduced from that first clue, in a kind of logical spiral.

Can you work out how I came to my conclusions?

'There's a lot of dust on your knees and elbows,' I said. 'And your fingers are also grubby. That implies you've been mucking around somewhere mucky. It's not mud or anything like that, just ordinary dust, so you've been indoors.'

'How do you know I don't walk around like this all the time?' said Amy.

'Those are expensive jeans you're wearing,' I said. 'If you were dusty all the time, like my friend Muddy, you'd wear scruffier clothes. And the fact that you're not usually dusty tells me you've probably been searching for something in dusty places. Under a bed, behind a desk, at the back of cupboards, that sort of thing.'

'And how could you tell I've been looking for something small?' said Amy,

'If you were looking for something large, you wouldn't have needed to go searching under a bed or in a cupboard, would you? You wouldn't get dusty elbows looking for a bike or a beach ball.'

Amy blinked at me, a disconcerted look on her face. 'And the rest? The fact that I think it's been stolen? The urgency thing?'

'Well, that's easy,' I said. 'The simple fact that you've come here to ask for my help tells me that you can't find this item and so you now think it was stolen. It must be precious to you, but not actually valuable, because you've come to me and not your parents or the police. Getting it back is a matter of urgency because you've obviously come here immediately, without bothering to even dust yourself down.'

Amy half-grinned, half-groaned. 'Which also tells you that it's only in the last couple of hours that I've given up looking.'

'Exactly. Easy.'

Amy sat back in my Thinking Chair, gawping at me as if I'd said something clever or unusual. 'Y'know, James Russell told me how you'd solved a mystery over at the museum. I thought he was exaggerating when he said you're the best detective ever.' (She was talking about the case of *The Pirate's Blood* – see volume three of my case files for details.)

'Well, umm, it's always nice to have a recommendation,' I blushed. 'But honestly, all I do is keep my eyes open. And my brain switched on. And my mouth shut. Well, sometimes. Anyway, I'm guessing that this item you've lost is perhaps jewellery? Or, possibly, judging again from your appearance, an expensive designer shirt?'

She frowned slightly. 'No. That's completely wrong.'

'Oh,' I said. I blushed again. 'Schoolbook?'

'No.'

'Oh. Phone?'

'No.'

'Oh. Camera?'

'No.'

'Oh. MP3 player packed with your complete collection of music and videos?'

'No.'

'Sorry, you're going to have to tell me,' I said weakly.

'It's, er, my diary.'

'Oh yeeees, of course,' I said, snapping my fingers. 'That would explain why . . . yes, sorry, carry on. Your diary?'

Now it was Amy's turn to blush. 'It's about the size of a paperback book. It has a chunky lock on it, and I've put my name in big letters across the front cover.'

'So, you've lost all your notes about when people's birthdays are coming up, and when you've got appointments at the dentist, that sort of thing? Why would anyone want to steal that?'

She blushed a bit more, the sort of red that's usually reserved for peppers and school sweatshirts.

'It's . . . not that sort of diary,' she said.

CHAPTER TWO

WHY? WHY? WHY WOULD ANYONE keep a diary? Not the birthdays-and-appointments-at-the-dentist type – that's OK, that's no problem. I mean the writing-down-stuff-you-don't-want-people-to-see type. A diary like that is *asking* for trouble. You just *know* that someone, sometime, is going to read it. I mean, if you don't want the world to discover your innermost thoughts – Don't. Write. Them. Down. I mean, arrgghhhh!

Ahem.

OK, I've calmed down again.

As Amy told me about her secret diary, grumbling thoughts such as those I've just mentioned went spinning round and round inside my head like a loose sock in a tumble dryer.

'This diary, then,' I said. 'It's something you keep quiet about?'

Amy nodded. 'Only my family know it exists. Not even my best friends know I keep it. I write in it most nights before I go to sleep. I put down all the classroom gossip. I write about all the secrets that my friends have told me and I write about what I think of everyone.'

She kind of winced as she spoke. I had the feeling that she realised what I was thinking.

'And, er, some of it isn't very . . . complimentary,' she said.

I let out a long, slow breath. I'd have quite liked to let out a long speech too, a speech which included several repetitions of the word 'why'. But I didn't.

'OoKaay,' I said. 'Tell me why you think it's been stolen.'

'On Thursday, after school, the other three people I'm doing this Twentieth Century thing with all came over to my house. We were going to get some of the artwork done.' (To explain: Mrs Penzler, our form teacher, had got the whole year group doing a huge project on twentieth century history. We'd been divided into small groups and given separate tasks to do. Amy's group was making a timeline wallchart, which was going to be put up all along the corridor outside our classrooms. I'd been given the job of writing some 'eyewitness' newspaper reports on various major events.)

'Who's in your group?' I said.

'Apart from me,' said Amy, 'there's Nicola Norris, Paul Welles and Kelly Fitzgerald.'

They were all kids from another class in our year group. I didn't know any of them very well, but none of these names jumped out at me waving a big sign saying 'Potential Diary Robber'.

'Whose idea was it to do this homework together at your house?' I said.

'Mrs Penzler's,' said Amy. 'Or, rather, she suggested we should work together. I volunteered to have the others over.'

'So are these three friends of yours?'

'No, quite the opposite,' said Amy. 'Mrs Penzler just stuck us together for this project because we're all good at art. Paul's obsessed with his collection of FrogWar figures, Nicola changes her likes and dislikes like the rest of us change underwear and Kelly's just a miserable moo.'

'I see,' I said. 'You think one of them swiped the diary on Thursday?'

'Yes. They all went home at about half past five. Then I went straight out with my mum, my dad and my older sister. We went for a pizza, then we went to the cinema. We didn't get back until late, so I went straight to bed and didn't even think about my diary. Yesterday morning, Friday, I was running late, so I never had a chance to notice the diary was gone. But last night, I went up to my room and no diary.'

'Do you always keep it in the same place?' I said.

'Always. It's on my window sill, under this sort of wooden pencil case thing I've got. I never put it anywhere else, ever. It's always under that pencil case. Nothing else had moved, the case included.'

'Are you sure one of your family haven't got it?' I said.

'They know,' said Amy sweetly, 'that if they so much as *touch* my diary, or breathe a word of its existence, I will tear them apart with my bare hands and rain hellfire and fury down upon them for all eternity.'

I thought for a moment. 'So, they're clear on that, then,' I nodded.

'I've spent all this morning searching,' said Amy. 'I've covered every square millimetre of my room, and every other room. I've even been poking behind the central heating radiators with a ruler. My diary is gone.'

I stood up and paced around a bit. Those paint pots were far too uncomfortable to sit on any longer.

'Do you still have the key?' I said.

'Yes,' said Amy. 'That was in my bedside cabinet. It's not been touched. The diary's lock is quite large, you'd have to rip half the cover off to force it open. But you'd only need a screwdriver, or something like that.'

I tapped at my chin in a particularly detective-y way.

'I still don't quite get what the *motive* for stealing it would be. *Why* would someone want your diary?'

Amy half-laughed. 'Well, that's obvious!' she spluttered. 'The contents are absolute dynamite! There'll be the most *incredible* rows if what I've written in there gets spread around school! Someone wants to cause some major trouble. Kelly would certainly be up for that, and I wouldn't put it past Nicola either. And Paul's a complete oddball who doesn't like me one little bit. Actually, some of the choicest comments in the diary are reserved for those three.'

'Even so,' I said, 'I really don't think that was what the thief had in mind. Well, probably not.'

'What makes you say that?' said Amy. 'They might even have *planned* to steal it!'

I had a logical reason to think that the theft was *not* carried out simply to create trouble at school. A reason based on the fact that the diary was taken on Thursday, and today was Saturday.

I also had a logical reason to think that the theft was definitely *not* planned.

Have you worked out my reasoning?

'You said you've kept your diary a secret,' I said. 'Nobody could have planned to steal it, because nobody knew it was there. Well, except your family.'

'So someone took it on impulse?' said Amy. 'They just happened to see it there?'

'Exactly,' I said. 'And I don't think they had troublemaking in mind for the simple reason that they've caused no trouble! They took the diary two days ago. You said it wouldn't be hard to force the lock open. And yet Friday has been and gone, a whole school day has passed during which the thief could have plastered the diary on every noticeboard from the Staff Room to the sports field. And yet, nothing.'

'I see what you mean,' said Amy. 'Perhaps the thief just wanted to be nosey?'

'And risk being found out, by stealing something that's *certain* to be missed?' I said. 'No, that doesn't seem quite right either. They'd have to be unbelievably nosey for that . . . Hmm, I just don't know . . .'

Amy sat forward on my Thinking Chair again. 'Can you help me? Please?'

'I'm almost tempted to say that anyone who writes a diary like that deserves all they get. But a crime has been committed, and crime is my business. Never fear, Saxby Smart is on the case!'

'What can I do to help?' said Amy.

'Well,' I said, 'assuming that one of these three *did* take the diary . . .'

'Nobody else has even visited the house all week, and my parents and sister have sworn on their lives they've never even been near it.'

' . . . then I'll need to establish the exact sequence of events at your house on Thursday afternoon. Could you write a detailed timetable for me by Monday morning?'

'Will do!'

After Amy had gone home, I slumped into my Thinking Chair. Now then, what should I do first? Get all this stuff put back into the shed? Or sit here and make some notes on the case?

No contest, really.

A Page From My Notebook

This case revolves around MOTIVE. Whoever took the diary must have had a REASON in mind.

Motive Problem 1: Nobody knew that the contents were, as Amy put it, 'absolute dynamite'. Obviously, anyone seeing a lock-up diary sitting there will think, Ooo, I wonder what she's put in that. You'd want to READ it. But would you then STEAL it? Wouldn't you at least have to have a strong suspicion that the diary WASN'T just the dentist-appointment-type diary, before you'd think it was worth stealing? I suppose having a lock on the diary would IMPLY that the contents might be gossipy, but the thief still couldn't possibly be sure.

Could the motive be BLACKMAIL? Steal the diary, then threaten Amy that the contents will be revealed to the whole school, unless she hands over cash. A lot of it.

Motive Problem 2: Same as Problem 1 above! To steal a diary because it MIGHT contain something blackmail-able still seems like a rather thin motive . . .

Odd Thought No.1: COULD someone else have known what sort of things Amy wrote in her diary? If they DID, this would eliminate these problems over motive.

BUT! Then we have another problem: how did they know about the diary when Amy had told nobody about it?

Odd Thought No.2: COULD a member of Amy's family have taken it after all? We still have the motive problem. BUT! Could there be something going on that I'm not yet aware of? Or that Amy herself isn't aware of?

What can we deduce so far about the thief? Only that they are impulsive: they took the diary on the spur of the moment. They clearly didn't think it through. They MUST have realised - at least by now - that there can only be a limited number of suspects in a case like this and that, therefore, there's a pretty good chance they'll be caught.

WAIT! Perhaps the thief HAS now realised this! What might their next move be? Could this have anything to do with the diary's contents not being made public on Friday?

One thing's for sure: the secrets Amy kept in that diary won't be secret any more! One twist of a screwdriver and that 'absolute dynamite' goes BOOM!

Chapter Three

ALONG THE MAIIN CORRIDOR AT school, outside a long run of classrooms (including mine), there are various noticeboards. One of them is a kind of free-for-all where pupils, parents and staff can put up info about out-of-school events, local stuff, that kind of thing. The Head once sold her house on that noticeboard, I'm told.

Anyway, on Monday morning I happened to spot two new announcements. The first one, declared:

HURRY! HURRY! HURRY!
Last few days! Mega-Sale MUST end Wednesday!
At SwordStore, Hanover Street
£££s off figures and construction kits
Meka-Tek 9000 – FrogWar – Gigablast – Ultra-X

(As readers of my earlier case files will know, I'd come across SwordStore before, and been hugely unimpressed.) The second new announcement was pinned so that it half-covered a request for charity donations and a thank you note from a mum who'd recently been in hospital. It said:

FOR SALE
'Encyclopedia Of British Crime Detection'
10 volumes – Good condition
Quick sale needed
Contact Harry Lovecraft, in Mrs Penzler's class.

My heart nearly skipped a beat, for two reasons. Firstly, because this was a rare set of books I'd read about ages ago, but had never been able to find. Secondly, because if I was going to get my eager little mitts on this important addition to my library, I'd have to deal with my arch enemy, that low-down rat Harry Lovecraft!

What a dilemma! Either I'd end up giving *money* to the world's slimiest slimeball, or I'd miss out on something I'd been wanting to get hold of for months.

I didn't feel in a dilemma for long. The lure of the books was too strong. All the way through the first lesson of the day, it was as if I could hear them calling to me: 'Buyyyy meeeee . . . Buuuuyyyyy mmmeeeee . . .'

I collared Harry Lovecraft when the bell went for

morning break.

'Well, well, Smart,' he oozed, 'I thought you'd be first in the queue. Ten points to me for a correct guess.'

He was looking even smarmier than usual. Shiny shoes, shiny black hair, shiny everything. I've said it before, and I'll say it again: add a thin, twirly moustache to his weasly upper lip and he'd be a Victorian villain!

'They're in good condition, are they?' I said.

'They're completely unread,' said Harry. 'Only a very dull person would find a tedious subject like that worth reading about.'

I bit my lip. 'How come you've got the complete set, then?'

'I haven't. My dad's having a clear-out. He's getting married again in a few months and we need to make space for his new wife's collection of shoes.'

'How many stepmothers does that make now?' I said. 'Three?'

'Four,' said Harry, with a smile like an eel. 'Nice girl. Can't see her lasting very long, though.'

I bit my lip again. 'Why do you need a quick sale? Are you into something dodgy again?'

'None of your business, Smart,' oozed Harry.

No, I thought to myself, I must give even a low-down rat like Harry Lovecraft the benefit of the doubt. I've been caught out like that before.

We agreed on a price. A remarkably fair one, amazingly enough! Purely by chance, I had some money in my pocket that day. I'd been given a ten pound note and strict orders to get three pints of milk and a loaf of bread on my way home. However, this was more important. I gave Harry the money and he said he'd bring the books into school with him tomorrow.

I was so pleased. Then I suddenly realised I'd almost forgotten about the missing diary. There were only a few minutes left before the next lesson, so I hurried to find Amy.

'Hi,' I said. 'Did you write down that timetable for me?'

'Yup,' she said, producing a folded sheet of paper from her pocket with a flourish. 'I've put down all the details I can remember.'

'Excellent,' I said. 'We'd better get back to class – the bell's about to go.'

We walked back together. We must have passed several dozen kids on the way, and I think Amy exchanged a few words with every last one of them! Every few seconds, it'd be, 'Hi, you coming to Abbie's party?' or, 'I'll see you at lunch, OK?' or, 'Give me a call, yeah?' No wonder she'd managed to cram her diary full of red-hot gossip and juicy secrets – her social network must have been more intricate than a spider's web.

Among those we passed were our three suspects in the theft of the diary, Nicola Norris, Paul Welles and Kelly Fitzgerald. Nicola was a tiny, sly-looking girl, who always reminded me of a chihuahua. Paul was never without his thick spectacles and a FrogWar Miniature Models catalogue sticking out of his blazer pocket, and Kelly was the sort who always wore her socks around her ankles and a scowl on her face.

To each of them Amy said, 'Have you got your stuff ready for art this afternoon?', and from each she got a 'Yes, no problem' or a 'Yeah, see you there'.

Something suddenly occurred to me. Something rather odd.

I pointed back over my shoulder. 'Our three suspects there,' I said. 'Did you speak to them on Friday?'

'Yes, and I spoke to them earlier on today, too,' said Amy. She lowered her voice to a whisper. 'Whichever one of them did it, they're playing it *very* cool. One of them is guilty, guilty, guilty, but you'd never know it.'

'Quite,' I said, frowning. 'They've been completely as normal with you? None of them has said anything odd, or given you a funny look, or behaved in any unusual way?'

'No,' said Amy. 'One hundred per cent as normal.'

'Assuming that one of those three *has* had your "dynamite" diary since last Thursday, doesn't a strange thought strike you? Something relating to how easy you said it would be to break the diary's lock, and how very explosive you said the diary's contents are?'

'No,' said Amy. 'What?'

Have you spotted an oddity in the way the suspects were acting towards Amy?

'I don't think the thief has actually *read* the diary,' I said.

'What?' spluttered Amy. 'That doesn't make sense. Steal a diary and not even *open* it?'

'Think about it,' I said. 'You and those three aren't exactly best buddies. You told me you'd even passed comment about them in the diary. One of them has had that diary for nearly four days. And yet all three, the thief included, continue to act completely normally towards you.'

Amy went pale. 'Yes, I see. If they'd read even a few pages of what I've written . . . And especially if they'd read what I'd written about them . . .'

'They'd have to be world-class experts in secret-keeping to carry on as normal. They'd be almost bound to react, even if it was in the tiniest of ways, just a weird look, or being a bit grumpy with you.'

'So,' said Amy, scrunching her face up in puzzlement, 'you're saying that as well as the thief *not* taking the diary in order to cause trouble . . . the thief *also* appears *not* to have taken the diary to even *read*?'

'Exactly!' I cried. 'I agree, it's very strange. But don't you realise? This is brilliant news!'

'Is it?' said Amy.

'Definitely,' I said. 'If the thief hasn't opened the diary, they haven't realised what dynamite they've got their hands on. All the secrets in there could still be completely safe! We haven't a moment to lose!'

Tracking down the culprit was now doubly urgent! It might still be possible to conclude this case without Amy's worst fears coming true and the whole school exploding into turmoil because of the contents of the diary!

Hurriedly, I unfolded the timetable Amy had written for me. I skipped through the information she'd put down.

'Where's this dining table you mention?' I said.

'At one end of the kitchen. Ground floor, at the back of the house.'

'And the bathroom is upstairs?'

'Yes, next to my room.'

'And your parents' bookshelves?'

'They're all along the top landing, from the door of my room to the door of their room.'

The bell for the next lesson rang. By now, Amy and I had arrived back at the classrooms. The lesson which followed was all about . . . er, something-or-other. I can't remember what. I was distracted by thinking about Amy's account of last Thursday afternoon.

This is what it said:

THURSDAY TIMETABLE
by Amy Parsons

Dear Saxby,
I can't be sure about the exact times of things, because I had no reason to keep looking at the clock. But these times are pretty good guesses, I think. The first and last times are spot on, because at those times I really did check the clock.

3:55 p.m. – Nicola, Paul, Kelly and I arrive at my house. My dad is back from work and he gets us all some drinks and some biscuits. Kelly scoffs half of them, greedy moo.

We are all at the dining table. We decide that this will be the best place to do our artwork, as it's the largest flat surface available. (I don't have a board or anything that's big enough to lay down on the carpet in my room.) Meanwhile, my dad reads in the living room; he doesn't come out.

4:15 p.m. – By now, we're working on our Twentieth Century Timeline. Nicola is doing up to World War I, Kelly is doing Europe Between The Wars, Paul is doing World War II, and I'm setting out The Cold War, Post-War Britain and The End Of The Soviet Union. Somehow, can't help thinking I've got the biggest job! Paul keeps asking everyone if they want to buy his old

CDs, because he's trying to get cash together to buy a load of FrogWar figures while they're cheaper.

'What, you mean instead of being jaw-droppingly overpriced, they're now just ridiculously overpriced?' I say. Paul glares at me! Can't he take a joke? Nicola asks, 'What CDs have you got?' Paul says, 'Mostly movie soundtracks, but I've got several FrogWar BattleBlast sound effects tracks to play while you're gaming'. Surprise, surprise, the rest of us say no thanks.

4:30 p.m. – Kelly scoffs the rest of the biscuits. Whole packet is now gone! Oinky pig! Paul still dribbling on about FrogWar. I ask him to can it.

Timeline looking rather good. We're pasting each completed section on to the back of a roll of wallpaper, so that we'll end up with one continuous picture. My drawing of the Berlin Wall is excellent. Hate to say it, but Paul's very good at drawing planes and soldiers.

4:45 p.m. – Nicola's illustrations of Edwardian people are going a bit wrong. I have flash of brains to the head and send her to my parents' bookshelves. There are a couple of big books there packed with old photos. She brings them down – they're ideal for copying!

Paul asks if we're sure we don't want to buy his old CDs. Kelly asks if there's any more biscuits. Answer to both questions is no.

4:50 p.m. – Kelly goes to the loo. I go to my school bag

(by the front door) to fetch pens. Work continues, Paul's dribbling on about FrogWar continues. To escape Paul's dribbling on about FrogWar, I pop up to my room to fetch some more sheets of coloured paper.

DIARY IS STILL THERE. I REMEMBER SEEING IT, IN ITS USUAL PLACE UNDER THE PENCIL CASE.

I return to the table. Kelly has helped herself to chocolate from the cupboard.

5:00 p.m. – Paul asks if any of us want to buy his old collection of sports car models. At this point, I lose patience with him. 'No, we don't,' I say, 'and we're all a bit fed up of you dribbling on about FrogWar too, so will you please button your lip and stop being such a loser!'

This shuts him up. At last. He glares at me again. Serves him right.

5:10 p.m. – We're all getting a bit tired of doing this now. Nicola takes the books back to the bookshelves. Kelly finishes her map of Europe and glues it on to the timeline. Nicola comes down a few minutes later and quickly starts packing stuff away in her bag.

Paul has spilled a load of ink on his hands. He goes up to the bathroom to wash it off. I give him the leftover coloured paper to put back on the way.

5:20 p.m. – We admire our handiwork. It's looking good. Nicola says she's in a hurry to get home. Kelly says she's in a hurry to get to the chip shop. Paul's being sulky. We roll the timeline up carefully and secure it with elastic bands.

5:25 p.m. – Nicola, Kelly and Paul all leave together. My mum and my sister arrive home at the same time, and we get ready to go out.

After that, you know the rest. Hope this helps.

Amy

It certainly did help. For one thing, it told me that Amy Parsons could be a bit of a moo herself, when she was in a mood. For another thing, it told me that *one* of the suspects was in the clear. Setting motive aside for a moment, there was one of the three who wouldn't have had the chance to steal the diary.

Can you work out which one of them was innocent?

All three of the suspects went upstairs at some point, either to the bathroom, to the bookshelves (both right next to Amy's room), or to Amy's room itself. However, Kelly did *not* go up there after Amy had seen her diary safe and sound. The other two *did* – Nicola to return the books, Paul to wash the ink off his hands and replace the spare coloured paper.

All three of them had the opportunity to do a bit of snooping and take the diary from Amy's window sill. But only Kelly was downstairs all the time *after* Amy had seen the diary. So Kelly had to be innocent.

As all this was swirling around in my head, the bell for the end of the lesson sounded. I suddenly realised I hadn't listened to a single word that had been said about . . . er, whatever-it-was.

Eliminating Kelly from my list of suspects was a big step forward. Since I'd realised that the diary probably hadn't been read yet (and that the whole case might still be tied up without the diary's contents becoming public), the urgency of the situation was the most important factor. So narrowing down the suspects to just two would be very helpful!

However . . .

What was still left unexplained was *why* the diary hadn't been read. Or, more to the point, why the thief still hadn't threatened Amy with blackmail, or posted the diary on the internet, or whatever other fiendish scheme they had in mind when they'd stolen the thing in the first place! It was all very puzzling.

For a while, I thought about another possibility. What if something accidental had happened to the diary? Something we hadn't accounted for up to now? *A-ha! That* would explain the strange lack of diary-reading/ blackmail/fiendish schemes, etc, etc.

But . . .

No, something accidental didn't really seem to fit the facts. I couldn't quite put my finger on exactly *why*, though.

My thoughts were interrupted by lunchtime. After a yummy, scrummy school dinner of burned thing, mushy thing and green thing (followed by spongy thing), I took a walk along the classroom corridor. I tried to pick up my thoughts where I'd left off.

They were interrupted again when Amy came bustling over to me. 'I've been thinking about another possibility,' she said. 'What if something accidental has happened to the diary? Something we haven't accounted for up to now?'

'I already thought of that,' I said. 'It doesn't really fit the facts. Although, I can't quite . . .'

'I think it might have fallen into the canal,' said Amy.

'Canal?' I said. 'What canal?'

'The houses in our street were once Victorian warehouses. The canal runs right along the back of them. If something fell out of my window it'd drop right into the water. My window was open on Thursday afternoon, and it was quite windy out. One hefty billow of the curtains and the diary on the window sill could easily have been knocked outside.'

I snapped my fingers. (Well, sort of – when I snap my fingers it makes more of a thud than a snap. Yet another little practical skill I'm rubbish at. Anyway, you know what I mean.)

Of course! *That* was why I couldn't quite put my finger on the reason that an accident didn't really fit the facts! I hadn't thought about precisely *where* the diary had been. Now I realised that an accident – like the one Amy had just described to me – was out of the question.

'Nooooo,' I said. Then I said 'nooooo' again, just to emphasise the point. 'That's not possible.'

'Why do you say that?' said Amy.

'Think back to what you've told me about exactly where your diary is kept,' I said.

Have you spotted why the diary couldn't have gone out of the window?

'You told me the diary is always under your wooden pencil case. Never anywhere else. If something accidental had happened to the diary, why hadn't it also happened to the pencil case? A billowing curtain, for example, couldn't lift up the pencil case, brush the diary out of the window and then replace the pencil case, could it?'

Amy sighed. 'Yes, I suppose it's obvious, really. I got my hopes up just then. Now I've got to go back to worrying. As soon as that diary gets opened . . .'

I stopped still.

Wait a minute! All this talk about accidents and previously-unseen-possibilities had suddenly kicked my brain into gear! Quickly, I took out Amy's Thursday timetable and read through it again.

'I think I've spotted a motive,' I said quietly, not taking my eyes off the timetable. 'At long last!'

'What motive?' said Amy.

I glanced at her. I didn't really want to say, not right at that moment, just in case I was wrong. The motive for the theft – if I was right – didn't exactly show Amy in a favourable light.

There was a clear difference between our two remaining suspects. One of them had a reason to be peeved at Amy, and the other didn't. And one of them had a possible motive for taking the diary, while the other didn't.

I was annoyed with myself for not spotting it before. Have you seen the evidence for a motive in that timetable too? No time to explain now – check if you're right when we get to the next chapter!

'Well?' said Amy.

'Got to go,' I said quickly, avoiding her gaze. 'There's not a moment to lose.' As I hurried off down the corridor, I called back to her over my shoulder, 'With a bit of luck, I'll have this sorted out by the end of school today.'

I headed for one of the classrooms close to the assembly hall. Now I had a definite plan. I would do three things:

1. Locate Suspect No.1.

2. Tell Suspect No.1 that the game was up and that I knew everything.

3. Get Suspect No.1 to hand over Amy's diary.

As it turned out, I needn't have bothered having a plan of any sort, definite or not. As I neared the classroom door, I was stopped in my tracks by the sound of a low, braying laugh.

I knew the sound all too well. It was the jeering sneer of that low-down rat Harry Lovecraft.

The classroom door was open a few centimetres. I crept up to it, carefully making sure that my shadow wouldn't pass across the crack of sunshine that sliced along the floor. Through the gap I could see Harry

Lovecraft sitting on one of the desks. He was talking to someone I couldn't see. They were alone in the classroom.

'Yes, I've got the money,' slimed Harry. 'I had some rubbishy old books to sell, and I knew exactly who'd take the bait.' He reached into his blazer and produced the money I'd paid him earlier that day. 'Here's your payment, courtesy of that revolting know-it-all, Saxby Smart.'

A hand appeared and took the cash. The unseen person said something I couldn't hear.

'Don't be an idiot,' said Harry Lovecraft. 'You think I want to be caught carrying it around? Drop it off where I told you. And make sure you do it before the end of school!'

Harry stood up and headed straight for the door. If I didn't get out of the corridor he'd see me in seconds!

I hopped on tiptoe, trying desperately not to let my shoes clack against the polished floor. I must have looked like a frog dancing on hot coals! A few bounding strides took me into the classroom next door and I crouched down out of sight.

I saw Harry slither past. Time to scuttle back out into the corridor, I thought to myself, and catch whoever it was Harry has been talking to.

But just as I was about to move, the bell for afternoon

lessons went. A trickle of kids started flowing outside the classrooms almost instantly. By the time I'd got into the corridor, the trickle had become a river. There was no hope of identifying the correct person now.

Never mind, I thought to myself, I've got a pretty good idea of who it was. Since overhearing Harry Lovecraft, I now also had a pretty good idea of exactly what had been going on all this time.

The whole case revolved around three things:

1. What was said at Amy's house on Thursday afternoon.

2. That mystery about why the thief seemed not to have read the diary.

3. The Mega-Sale at the local branch of SwordStore in Hanover Street.

I hurried along back to class.

'Drop it off where I told you,' Harry had said.

So . . . Where might that be, I wondered?

CHAPTER FOUR

OUTSIDE OUR CLASSROOMS, NEXT TO the racking where people put their lunchboxes and assorted other stuff, there is a long honeycomb of lockers. I have no idea why these are called 'lockers' because they have no locks on them, just lift-up wooden hatches. Every pupil is allocated one; mine is on the third row up, fourth from the end.

We use them to store school books, homework, and so forth. Teachers use them now and again to distribute stuff like newsletters and parental consent forms.

Most people drop by their locker at the end of the day, which was why I was standing beside the lockers when the bell went for the end of school. I positioned myself in front of Harry Lovecraft's, top row, second from the left.

'Are you getting in my way for a reason, Smart?' smarmed Harry. 'Or are you just being your normal awkward self? I told you, I'll bring those books in for you tomorrow.'

'There's a definite reason,' I said. 'This won't take long.'

As Amy emerged from the classroom I flagged her down and asked her to round up Nicola, Paul and Kelly for me. A couple of minutes later, we were all gathered together beside the lockers.

I could see Mrs Penzler, our form teacher, marking homework at her desk with huge swishes of her pen. I considered calling her over too, but I decided that this matter was probably best dealt with amongst the six of us.

'What's this about?' said Nicola. 'I've got netball practice in ten minutes.'

'I've got to get to the shops,' said Paul.

'And I've got a steak and kidney pie sitting at home with my name on it,' grumbled Kelly.

'Last Thursday afternoon,' I began, 'Amy here had her diary stolen from her room at home.'

'What's that got to do with us?' said Nicola.

'I didn't even know she had a diary,' grumbled Kelly.

'Get to the point, Smart,' sneered Harry Lovecraft. 'You're boring me already.'

'The point is,' I said, 'that only one of you three, Nicola, Paul and Kelly, could have taken it. I was able to rule Kelly out of my investigations, so the theft had to be down to either Nicola or Paul. Now, at this point, Amy, I really do have to say that, in a way, you brought this entire affair on yourself.'

'What?' she cried. She shook her head in astonishment. 'What?'

'It was all a question of motive,' I said. 'It's no secret that Amy, Nicola, Paul and Kelly aren't best buddies. They're just having to work together on this history project we're all doing. But you'd need more than that to have a motive to actually steal Amy's diary. And Amy gave you that motive . . . Paul.'

Paul stared at me like a small furry animal caught in the crosshairs of a shotgun. He went paler than a slice of white bread.

'Umm . . .' he said at last, trembling.

'We all know,' I said, 'that Paul's a huge FrogWar fan. He collects all the figures and builds all the weaponry and stuff. Yes?'

'Yes,' said Paul quietly.

'If you look at the noticeboard further along this corridor, you'll see that there's a sale on at SwordStore, which stocks the whole FrogWar range. FrogWar merchandise isn't cheap. A money-off sale is something Paul *really* doesn't want to miss. But it ends this Wednesday. So what's Paul been doing? Saving up as hard as he can, trying to sell some old CDs, doing his best to raise enough cash by this Wednesday to get a few bargains.

'Last Thursday afternoon, he asked his fellow timeline-assemblers if they were interested in any of the stuff he was selling. They weren't. Unfortunately, Paul maaaaay have asked them one too many times, and he maaaaay have chattered on a bit about FrogWar in general. His fellow timeline-assemblers maaaaay have found this slightly irritating.

'However, Amy's response was a little harsh. In fact, she was positively rude to Paul, and even called him a loser. Which, completely understandably, made him very cross. If someone who didn't like reading crime stories the way I do started moaning about them and calling me a loser, I expect I'd get pretty annoyed too.

'A short while later, an opportunity for revenge presents itself. He's returning some coloured paper to Amy's room when he notices her diary. People always value their diaries, he thinks to himself, even if the only thing they put in them is a note or two about the weather.

'He wants to raise some money, and quickly. I'll hold that diary to ransom, thinks Paul. Now, bear in mind that Paul's angry with Amy. He's not in the clearest-thinking of moods. He sneaks the diary away . . . er, in his pocket?'

Paul looked sheepish. 'Tucked under my sweatshirt,' he muttered.

'Tucked under his sweatshirt,' I said. 'But as soon as he gets home, he realises how stupid he's been. He's no thief. He's not the sort of person who normally goes around stealing other people's property. He feels terrible about it. But what can he do?

'The right thing to do, of course, would be to simply return the diary to Amy. But she's made it absolutely clear what she thinks of him. If I return it, thinks Paul, I'll have to admit what I've done. Amy can't stand me. She'll make sure I get into a whole heap of trouble for this.'

'So, Paul simply hangs on to the diary for a couple of days. It's locked, and he doesn't want to open it, but he knows he's got to get rid of it somehow. Why not just throw it away? That's one obvious solution, but it doesn't solve his other problem: getting money together for the FrogWar sale.

'And now Paul gets another idea. A very sneaky and unpleasant one. But, he reasons, Amy's been mean to him, so perhaps she deserves to be taught a lesson after all. Paul goes to see Harry Lovecraft. Everyone in this school knows that if there's anything sneaky and unpleasant to be done, Harry Lovecraft likes to have a hand in it.'

Harry took a step closer to me. 'Watch what you're saying, Smart,' he growled.

'So Paul goes to see Harry Lovecraft,' I said, keeping my eyes firmly on Harry. 'And he says to Harry, "I've got someone's personal diary for sale. Are you interested?" "I might be," says Harry. "What's in it?" "Don't know," says Paul. "It's locked, but the lock can be easily broken."

'Harry has a think. A locked diary, eh? That might contain all sorts of embarrassing stuff. Stuff he can blackmail the diary's owner with. Is it worth risking a few pounds? Yes, why not? Naturally, Harry doesn't want to spend his *own* money on the diary, so he decides to have a sale of his own. He puts up a notice on the board offering some books he knows I'll be interested in.

'Not knowing what's going on, I fall for it and I buy the books. Now Harry's got some money for the diary. At the end of lunchtime today, he meets with Paul in that classroom up the corridor there and gives him the cash. Paul offers to hand over the diary.

'"Don't be an idiot," says Harry. "Drop it off where I

told you. And make sure you do it before the end of school." I overheard that conversation. So, I think to myself, Paul's supposed to drop the diary off somewhere *at* school, because Harry's expecting to pick it up before going home. Where could this somewhere be? It must be somewhere accessible to both Paul and Harry, but also somewhere that it probably wouldn't be spotted. Somewhere Harry could retrieve it without looking at all suspicious.'

I turned around and tapped on the door of Harry's locker. 'The only place I could think of,' I said, 'was these lockers.'

I looked at the five of them, standing there, and the five of them looked back at me.

'If I'm right about all this,' I said, 'then inside this locker is Amy's stolen diary.'

'You're wrong,' scoffed Harry. 'Whatever you think you overheard, you totally misunderstood. Paul was selling me those old CDs you mentioned. Nothing more than that.'

'Really?' I said. 'What were their titles?'

Harry glared at me. 'None of your business, Smart. We're all getting fed up of you poking your nose in where it's not wanted.'

'If it's just CDs,' said Amy, 'you won't mind if Saxby takes a look.'

'If I'm wrong,' I said with a shrug, 'you get to see me make a fool of myself. I can't believe you'd miss the chance of that.'

Harry made a kind of half-tut noise. I spun around and opened the locker door. Sitting on top of a pile of books and papers was a lock-up diary with the words *My Diary by Amy Parsons* written in felt tip across the cover. Amy bounded forward, hand outstretched, but Harry blocked her way.

'Give it back!' cried Amy.

'If you lost it, then it's mine now,' sneered Harry. 'Finders keepers, as they say. Losers weepers. I paid good money for it. If you've got any complaints, talk to Paul.'

Amy, Nicola, Paul and Kelly all started talking at once. I raised a hand for silence.

'OK,' I said in a low voice. 'You keep it, Harry. But if that's what you decide to do, I'll have no choice but to let Mrs Penzler know what's been happening. She's just over there, marking homework.'

Harry's snake-eyes slid from me to the nearby classroom and back again.

'Is opening that diary really worth the trouble you'll get into?' I said. 'Are you willing to risk the consequences, for a diary that's got nothing in it but people's birthdays and a few reminders? That's all it contains, isn't it, Amy?'

'Yes, er, that's all,' said Amy hastily. 'That's all. But I want it back. I'll never remember another birthday if I don't have it.'

Harry stared at me, like a leopard staring at its prey, wondering when to pounce. 'You're lying,' he growled.

'Am I?' I whispered. 'Are you going to take that chance?'

For a second, I really thought he was going to slam the locker shut and send us all packing. But then he reached in, picked the diary up and flung it carelessly at Amy.

She caught it mid-spin. Immediately, she pulled out a small key from her blazer pocket, opened the diary, and started to tear out the pages. She ripped them into tiny shreds, dumping the lot into the waste paper bin that stood just inside the entrance to the classroom. Then she took a carton of orange juice from her bag, ripped off the top and soaked the shreds into a sticky pulp.

'How are you going to remember people's birthdays now?' asked Kelly.

Amy dropped the empty carton into the bin. 'Thank goodness for that. That's one mistake I won't be making again.'

Harry's face flushed through half a dozen shades of

purple fury. 'You *were* lying,' he spat.

'You really think I'd go to all this trouble for an appointments book?' I said.

Paul approached Amy, his feet shuffling uneasily and his eyes looking everywhere except straight ahead. 'Amy, I'm sorry, I really am.' He handed her the money he'd got from Harry. 'This is the very least I owe you, as well as an apology.'

'Yes, well,' said Amy, 'I, er, shouldn't have been so rude to you.'

Mrs Penzler's voice boomed from inside the classroom. 'You six! Don't you have homes and after-school clubs to go to? Off you go! Chop chop! Don't make me come out there!'

We all headed off down the corridor, Harry stomping along in a cloud of suppressed rage. He jabbed me on the shoulder. 'Don't get too smug, Smart,' he hissed. 'The day's coming when I'll get my own back on you. And it's coming sooner than you think.'

He marched on ahead. I smiled to myself. 'Oh, Harry!' I called, before he stormed out of sight. 'Don't forget our deal. I'll expect those books in the morning? OK?'

He looked daggers at me for a moment, then stalked away, muttering under his breath.

I walked home, making plans to sit in my Thinking Chair and write up my notes on the case. It was only when I arrived at my shed that I remembered I'd left its entire contents strewn across the lawn. Oh, I thought. Better get to work.

Case closed.

Case File Twelve:

Whispers from the Dead

CHAPTER ONE

ADULTS CAN BE STUPID. I mean really, seriously dum-dum stupid. They fight over the most ridiculous things, they invade each other's countries and they make TV shows containing no jokes or car chases.

It's the weird things they're prepared to *believe* which baffle me most: they read horoscopes, buy celebrity gossip magazines and listen to weather forecasts. You'd think they didn't have a molecule of common sense between them.

In my files are notes on a case I've labelled *Whispers From the Dead*. It's a perfect example of how, sometimes, adults have to be saved from their own utter idiocy. It all started a couple of days after the events described in *Diary of Fear*.

Since the previous weekend, I'd taken everything out of the garden shed, my Crime HQ. I'd chucked away a few broken bits and pieces, and put the rest back in again. I'd made absolutely sure that I was putting everything back in the most space-saving way possible: garden hose neatly coiled, lawnmower hung up on a big hook, paint tins carefully stacked according to size, and so on. I badly needed more space for my desk, my files and my Thinking Chair. It was bad enough being forced to share the shed with all that DIY and gardening stuff, but having to shove it out of the way all the time was adding insult to injury, as they say.

However, now that everything was back inside the shed, I was beginning to wonder what exactly had gone wrong with my tidy-up plan. There seemed to be even less room in there than before! It didn't make sense. Had someone sneaked along in the middle of the night and added the contents of their shed to mine? The gardening gear was now teetering in a massive pile, which looked like it was about to fall over and bury all my files under half a tonne of plant pots. My desk *would not* sit straight! One side was higher than the other, its legs propped up on a box of paint brushes. And the only way I could even fit my Thinking Chair in was to turn it one hundred and eighty degrees, so it faced the door. It just looked completely wrong!

I was scrambling over the top of the desk (and suddenly realising that it blocked off the drawers of my filing cabinet) when there was a knock at the door.

'Come in!' I called. Or, rather, 'Mff eeen!' because I was rapidly slipping down the gap between the edge of the desk and the back of the chair.

I heard the door open, and then the unmistakable sarcasm of my great friend Izzy sliced through the dusty air. 'Do you point your bum at everyone who comes in here, or is it just me?'

'Hummlee erp, um sperkk,' I groaned. I think the way my hand was waggling wildly behind my back must have been what told Izzy I was saying, 'Help me up, I'm stuck'. She took hold of the waistband of my trousers and hauled me free. I sat on my desk, flapping dust out of my hair. My glasses were dangling off one ear.

'I've been rearranging things,' I gasped.

'Why?' said Izzy, raising that trademark arched eyebrow of hers. 'Weren't you cramped enough in here before?'

'I think the paint pots have been cloning themselves,' I said. 'I can't get it all to fit.'

'Why have you got your Thinking Chair facing the

door?' said Izzy. 'It just looks completely wrong.'

'Yes, I know,' I wailed. 'I don't understand it.'

She clambered over the chair and joined me on the desktop. She perched by the shed's perspex window, clearing herself a space in the dust before she sat down.

I stared at the floor-to-ceiling jumble around me. I suppose it's not just adults who can be really, seriously, dum-dum stupid. Even brilliant schoolboy detectives like me get it wrong sometimes.

'I've got a case for you,' announced Izzy.

'Perfect,' I said gratefully. 'Anything to avoid having to think about this hideous mess for a while. How can I help?'

Izzy, the school's in-house genius and my Chief Research Brainbox, had helped me out on many past investigations. But this was the very first time she'd brought a new case to my attention. I was eager to hear the details.

'Do you know The Pig and Fiddle?' she said. 'The big building in the centre of town?'

'Er, yes, the pub? Didn't you once tell me your relatives run it?'

'That's right, my uncle and aunt have owned it for about ten years. It's a sort of pub, restaurant and hotel all in one. It's got a very good reputation. They've had tourists from all over the world staying there, because of all the nearby castles and historic sites.'

'I think I've seen adverts for the place,' I said. 'Don't they have a theatre attached to it or something?'

'Not quite,' said Izzy. 'One end of the pub part is a large stage. My uncle books all sorts of acts for evening performances. Comedians, pop groups, speciality acts, that sort of thing.'

'What's a speciality act?' I said.

'Oh, the more oddball stuff,' said Izzy. 'You know, sword swallowers, dancing dogs, jugglers. A few months ago they had a couple of absolutely brilliant quick change artists, who could zip through different costumes like lightning. Really clever.'

'So these acts are a sort of daily show?' I said.

'Every evening at eight o'clock, yes. Some acts are only on for one night, some get booked for a couple of weeks or more. My uncle won't let anyone else deal with the bookings – he loves all that. I think he really wanted to be a circus ringmaster!'

'And I assume something's gone wrong for one of these acts? Is that why you're here?'

'Not exactly,' said Izzy. She hesitated, and her voice became quieter. 'There's a performer called Godfrey Frye. He's been touring abroad for ages, apparently, and has never been here before. He's been appearing at the nightly show for the past few days and he's booked up until the end of next week.'

'And . . .?'

'And he's the creepiest person on the face of the earth!'

I shrugged. 'Well, there's no law against being weird, thank goodness.'

'He's a clairvoyant, a medium. He picks people out of the audience and starts seeing into their future.'

'Sure, I've seen similar stage acts on TV,' I said.

Izzy shook her head. 'There's more to it than that. I went to last night's show with my mum. This Godfrey Frye started talking about *me*. I'd never so much as set eyes on him before, but he knew things he couldn't *possibly* have guessed. What's more, he knew about *you*!'

'Huh?'

'He said he's communicated with spirits and been told your name. "A friend who fights crime," he said. "You have a friend called Saxby." If he'd said, "You have a friend called Tom," or, "You have a friend called Sam," well, that's nothing, is it? That could just be guesswork. But *your* name?'

'And did he predict my future?' I said.

'Yes, he did. And I'm really scared.'

'Why?'

'Because,' said Izzy, 'he said your future was filled with failure and mistakes. He said he heard the voices of the dead speaking to him, and they've told him you're heading for disaster!'

Chapter Two

'Hang on a minute,' I said. 'Let's . . . I mean . . . Couldn't . . . Hang on a minute.'

I suddenly felt as if my nervous system had been put through a shredder. It's a pretty terrifying experience to . . . be told that . . . in your future . . .

I batted my hands about to shoo away such ridiculous thoughts. 'Oh, come *on*!' I cried. 'It's a stage act! It's all fake, it's a trick.'

'If he's a fake,' said Izzy, 'he's the best bloomin' fake I've ever seen.'

'Good grief,' I cried, 'you're the most sensible, intelligent person I know. How can you let yourself be fooled by such nonsense?'

'Normally, I *would* say it was nonsense. You know me.

You know I don't believe in astrology and superstitions, and all that mystical rubbish. But you weren't there last night. I'm beginning to wonder whether I've been right or not. *How* could he know about me? And you? *How?*'

'Weeeeeeell,' I said. I pondered for a moment or two. 'OK, I don't know, but one thing's for certain: he is *not* getting messages from beyond the grave!'

Izzy sighed. She slumped, chin in hand, looking thoroughly miserable. 'You're right,' she said, after another couple of sighs. 'I'm being really silly. But I'm telling you, Godfrey Frye would give a block of concrete the jitters. He's frightening. Never mind the audiences, he's got half the *staff* at The Pig and Fiddle convinced he's for real. The waiters in the restaurant talk about him in hushed whispers. And my uncle is the worst one of the lot!'

'How so?'

Izzy let out a long, slow breath through her teeth. She sounded like a paddling pool deflating. 'Uncle Raphael is the reason I'm here. He's always been gullible. He'll believe whatever people tell him. He once got suckered by a crook who was pretending to be from the gas company. The man got away with the entire contents of the pub's till.'

'And he believes that Godfrey Frye really can talk to the dead and see into the future?'

'Incredible as it sounds, yes,' said Izzy. 'And from what I hear, Godfrey Frye does nothing to contradict that impression. He claims he's totally genuine. Well, he would, wouldn't he? I'm getting worried. You see, normally, Aunt Mina's around to give my uncle a kick up the backside and point out when he's being a complete idiot. But she's away at the moment. Her sister's been ill and she's looking after her.'

'When's she coming back?'

'Nobody's sure. She's in New Zealand.'

'Oh, I see. Can't she give your Uncle Raphael a kick up the backside over the phone?'

'My cousins haven't told her. They don't want her to worry, what with her sister's illness and everything.'

'Cousins?' I said.

'Yes, there are six of them,' said Izzy. 'They and Aunt Mina and Uncle Raphael all live on the top floor, above the hotel. The eldest two work in the restaurant.'

'What do they think about Godfrey Frye?'

'Half of them agree with me,' said Izzy, 'but he won't listen to them.'

'What about the other half?' I said.

'Hah! The other half are equally convinced Frye is a genuine psychic!'

'Couldn't you get someone else to deliver this kick up the backside? Your parents; someone like that?'

'You don't know Uncle Raphael,' said Izzy. 'The only person he'll *ever* take advice from is my Aunt Mina. He's almost as stubborn as he is gullible.'

'But what exactly do you think Godfrey Frye will do?' I said. 'Steal from the till too?'

'It's not a question of what *he* will do,' said Izzy sadly. 'It's Uncle Raphael. Any other time, I might leave the whole situation well alone and let Raphael believe whatever he likes. But just recently, he's been talking about the Big Holiday Fund. Apparently, it's almost complete.'

'What's the Big Holiday Fund?' I asked.

'The family have been planning a trip to Florida, for all eight of them. Three weeks, all the theme parks, the lot. They've been saving up for years. Literally, years. This holiday is going to cost a small fortune.'

'And now this small fortune is nearly ready to spend?'

'Right. Any other time, if Uncle Raphael wanted to believe in some fortune-telling mystic, I'd say let him. If he wants to make himself look a twerp, fine. But right now, with a small fortune in his pocket . . .'

'Yes,' I said, chewing at my lip. 'Looks like a recipe for trouble, doesn't it?'

'He's been dropping hints about some sort of huge payoff, some get-rich-quick scheme he's thought up, and how they'll soon be able to afford a holiday in Florida every year. I have no idea what this scheme might be, but I don't like the sound of it one little bit. And I just *know* my uncle's going to get Godfrey Frye involved in it.'

I pondered for a moment or two, narrowing my eyes detective-style. 'What sort of get-rich-quick scheme would somebody think up that needed a clairvoyant? One that involves knowing the outcome of something in advance, right?'

'Yes, that's logical,' said Izzy.

'Does your uncle go in for gambling?'

'What, you mean horses, cards, that sort of thing? Good grief, no. He thinks gambling is for total losers. He won't even do the National Lottery. Aunt Mina says it's the only sensible opinion he's got!'

'Perhaps it's to do with stocks and shares, or changes in different world currencies?' I said. 'People chance money on unknown outcomes there, don't they?'

'I think it's highly unlikely,' said Izzy. 'Raphael has trouble paying his bills on time, let alone understanding international financial markets.'

'Predictions of "failure, mistakes and disaster" in my future, eh?' I muttered. 'Well, let's see if this Godfrey Frye is right, shall we? Save me a seat at tonight's show.'

'Sure!'

'And in the meantime, see what other information you can find about all that voices-from-beyond stuff in general. Start with Sir Arthur Conan Doyle, who wrote the Sherlock Holmes stories. I'm sure I read in my ten-volume *Encyclopedia of British Crime Detection* that he got involved with mystics and mediums.'

'And while I'm doing that,' said Izzy, clambering back over my Thinking Chair, 'you can get this shed sorted. I'll see you later!'

A Page From My Notebook

This Godfrey Frye person is a mystery in more ways than one. For one thing, his 'powers' MUST be down to trickery – if they weren't, he'd hardly be wasting them on a nightly performance at The Pig And Fiddle, would he? And yet . . .

- How DID he get to know about me? WAS it all guesswork?
- Did he get the info from Izzy? Did she let something slip that she wasn't aware of?
- A-HA! Could he have read one of my earlier volumes of case files? Hmm, probably not. Even if he had, how could he have known in advance that Izzy was in the audience?
- In any case, why concern himself with ME at all?

BUT! The Immediate Problem is Izzy's uncle.

- Even if Frye is a total phoney, it doesn't mean he's daft (except for claiming he's not a phoney)! Perhaps he'll turn down any involvement in this get-rich-quick scheme. Could Izzy be worrying for nothing?
- What IS this get-rich-quick scheme Izzy's uncle has got planned? And how at risk is the Big Holiday Fund?

My Plan Of Action:

1. See Frye's act and spot the trickery.
2. Find out what this mysterious scheme is and stop Izzy's uncle making a terrible mistake.

CHAPTER THREE

THE PIG AND FIDDLE IS a large, impressive building on the corner of the market square. The main road through town runs past it on one side, and on the other is the first in a long line of tall houses.

The whole of the outside is cleanly whitewashed, with a series of curling vines painted as a mural around the main entrance. A rectangular pub sign, showing a balloon-like piggy-wiggy dancing and playing the violin, juts out over the pavement, about four metres off the ground. Below it on the wall is a glass-enclosed board, on which are pinned details of the acts currently appearing in the nightly show, special offers in the restaurant and a couple of pictures of rooms in the hotel.

I met Izzy and her mum under the sign. Izzy's mum is just like her daughter in the same way that a small piece of cheese is just like the Sydney Opera House. In other words, not one tiny little bit. Isobel is all sparkly T-shirts and jangling bangles. Her mother always looks severe and no fun. That evening, she was wearing a business suit which said, 'Don't mess with me, buster', and said it very loudly.

'So, you think something dodgy is going on too, do you, Saxby?' said Izzy's mum.

'We'll just have to wait and see,' I said.

We made our way into the pub. It was a very large room filled to capacity with tables and chairs. There was thick red carpet on the floor and the gleam of brass was all over the place. Over at the far end was a raised area, screened off by a curtain and lit by stage lights suspended from the ceiling.

The place was busy. I estimated around a hundred and fifty people were sitting at the tables, or at the long, shiny bar. Several family groups were scoffing chicken and chips or vegetable lasagne. I even recognised one or two kids from school.

We found a table quite close to the stage. Izzy's mum went to buy us a round of orange juice and Izzy told me about the research she'd been doing earlier on.

'You were right about Sir Arthur Conan Doyle,' she

said. 'In the late nineteenth and early twentieth centuries, there was a lot of interest in clairvoyants and messages from beyond the grave. They called it spiritualism and Conan Doyle was a big fan. There was a famous magician and escape artist at the time called Houdini. He was friendly with Conan Doyle at first, but they fell out because Houdini kept on exposing various clairvoyants as tricksters. There's a very long history of magic tricks being sucessfully passed off as psychic powers.'

'Did you manage to find anything out about Godfrey Frye?' I said, above the clanking of knives and forks from a nearby table.

'Nothing at all,' said Izzy. 'There are loads of people doing an act like this and they all seem to advertise on the net, but Godfrey Frye isn't even mentioned. Anywhere.'

'Interesting,' I said. 'That suggests he doesn't like attracting attention. I wonder why.'

Someone who certainly *did* like attracting attention was a weirdly dressed man at the bar. He was wearing a pair of drainpipe jeans which looked like they'd been washed in a cement mixer, and a ripped shirt which had *Oi!* in huge green letters on the front and a garish splash of red on the back. He was nattering away to a knot of adults gathered around him, who all seemed to be laughing excessively at his jokes. One of this group was . . . good grief, was that Izzy's mum?

'Yes, it is,' groaned Izzy. 'He's why she was happy to come here again tonight.'

'Who is he?' I said.

'You'll find out,' said Izzy, with a look on her face identical to the look an adult gives a toddler when it starts screaming in the middle of a supermarket.

A man in a smart dinner jacket came bustling over to us. He was round and bald, with a thin, pointy moustache poised delicately above a beaming smile. He reminded me of something I'd seen recently, but I couldn't quite think what.

'Izzy-Wizzy!' he cried in a deep voice. Izzy flinched and the embarrassed expression on her face intensified for a moment. 'Back again tonight? Did our maestro of the mystical arts impress you, then?'

'Something like that,' said Izzy. 'This is my friend Saxby. Saxby, this is my Uncle Raphael.'

'Hi,' I said.

'The famous detective!' cried Uncle Raphael. 'Delighted to meet you, young sir, delighted!' He grasped my hand and shook it until I thought it might come loose. 'No doubt you're also here to witness the many marvels of Mr Frye?'

'Absolutely,' I said. 'I've heard so much about him. And you, in fact.'

(Ah, that was it! Uncle Raphael reminded me of that sign outside the pub.)

'Excellent! All good, I hope!' declared Uncle Raphael. 'Is your mother here, Izzy? Oh yes, there she is! Good grief, old Jimmy certainly draws a crowd, doesn't he!'

'Uncle Raphael,' said Izzy, 'we need to talk to you about Godfrey Frye. And about this payoff you've mentioned to my cousins.'

Uncle Raphael's eyes darted around the room, then he swung himself into a chair beside us. 'Shhh! It's still all hush-hush. I haven't mentioned a word to our Mr Frye about it yet. I tell you, it's the most fabulous idea I've ever had. Can't wait to put it into action.'

'Yes, but what *is* it?' asked Izzy.

Uncle Raphael, grinning broadly, tapped his nose and winked. 'It's brilliant, that's what it is. I thought I'd have a word with Mr Frye after he's played his set tonight. You know, show him the basics of the idea. I think he's more amenable at that hour, more open to suggestions. He says after a session with the spirits his mind is a misty tangle of weariness.'

'OK,' said Izzy. 'But. What. Is. It?'

If Uncle Raphael had grinned any more broadly, his lower jaw would have been in danger of falling off. He wiggled his eyebrows in delight. 'Let's just say, chaps, that someone is arriving at this hotel in a couple of days' time who presents me with a once in a lifetime opportunity. Everything is suddenly coming together.'

He stood up to leave. 'Must press on! Duty calls!'

'Could I meet Godfrey Frye?' I said. 'Is he around at the moment?'

'Yes, he'll be in the artistes' green room,' said Uncle Raphael. 'I'm not sure he likes being disturbed before he contacts the spirits, you know, says it interferes with his perceptive aura. Still, we can ask. I'm sure he'd make an exception for a fan.'

'Remind me,' I said to Izzy. 'What did he say about me? Can you remember his exact words?'

'I think so,' said Izzy. 'He said, "You have a friend called Saxby. A friend who fights crime. I see him. The spirits show his face to me. They show me his future and it is filled with failure and mistakes. He is heading for disaster." Yes, I'm sure that's exactly what he said.'

'Should you really be out tonight, Saxby?' asked Uncle Raphael fearfully. 'What if this disaster happens to you sooner rather than later?'

'I'll take the risk,' I said flatly.

Uncle Raphael led me on a weaving route around the tables. I glanced back at Izzy and she gave me a quick thumbs-up.

'By the way,' I said. 'Don't tell Mr Frye who I am.'

'Oh?' said Uncle Raphael. 'Why's that?'

'Well, er, he might get a psychic shock, you know, if he realises I'm the one he's predicted all that doom and gloom for. It might send his perceptive aura out of whack or something. I'll break it to him gently who I am.'

'Of course, I see,' said Uncle Raphael. 'Yes, that's very considerate of you. He's a sensitive man. He's in tune with the cosmic mysteries, the balance of his delicate inner peace can be upset by the smallest movement in the space-time continuum. He was telling me about it over a pie and a pint the other night.'

We went through a small lobby area and down a dimly lit corridor. At the end of it was a door marked *Private. Artistes Only*. Uncle Raphael knocked gently.

'Mr Frye?' he said softly. 'Enormous apologies for interrupting your meditations, but I have a youngster here who's dying to meet you. A fan. Might he be permitted a few moments of your time?'

There was a long silence. Not the slightest sound came from inside the room.

'Naturally, we could return at another time if the spirits are currently occupying your attention,' said Uncle Raphael, with just a trace of a tremor in his voice.

There was another long silence. And then, like the sound of a slowly creaking hinge in the dead of night, there came a voice. It was rasping and scratched, a quivering, horror movie voice that turned my spine to ice.

'You may enter.'

Uncle Raphael bustled the two of us into the room. At first, I couldn't see Godfrey Frye. The only light came from a small, heavily shaded table lamp, which threw a hazy circular glow up on to the ceiling. Half the room seemed to be filled with an acrid mist, which it took me a few seconds to realise was cigarette smoke.

At last, Godfrey Frye emerged from the smoke. He stood up from a sofa on the other side of the room and advanced towards me, like a sailing ship gliding out of a midnight fog.

Izzy had been right. I'd never seen anyone so instantly frightening in all my life. He was short, and so unnervingly thin that he looked like he was walking out of a distorting mirror. His jet black hair was greased back over his bumpy head and his cheeks were sunken and lined. His skin was like the wrappings on an Egyptian mummy, making his red, slit-like mouth and his piercing green eyes stand out all the more.

If I'd been a cartoon character, I'd have done a loud g-g-gulp at that moment. As it was, I felt my every last gram of confidence suddenly drain away through my wobbly legs.

'You wish to see me?' said Godfrey Frye in his slow, grating whisper. He took a long drag from the cigarette that was held delicately between his elongated, bony fingers.

'Umm . . . yes . . . hello,' I said weakly.

Uncle Raphael bounced over to Godrey Frye, who didn't take his gaze off me for a single second. 'Glad I could see you before the show, old man,' said Uncle Raphael. 'I was wondering if I might have a word with you later on?'

'Unless it is concerning my overdue wages, Mr Moustique,' said Godrey Frye slowly, 'then I fear I may not be available.'

'Ah,' said Uncle Raphael. 'Well, it is about a very important financial matter. Very important. Won't take more than a moment of your valuable time . . .'

There was another long silence. Godfrey Frye didn't move a muscle. 'Very well,' he said at last.

'Excellent!' cried Uncle Raphael. 'Top notch! Well, break a leg 'n' all that. Toodle-oo!'

He scooted off. A drifting trail of pungent smoke gradually escaped Godfrey Frye's mouth and he returned to his sofa.

'Who are you, boy?' he said.

And in that moment, I knew he was a phoney. Whatever hold he had over his audiences, or over the staff of The Pig and Fiddle, I was clear in my own mind that everything he did was down to careful trickery.

Have you spotted why?

He didn't know who I was. He had, so he'd told Izzy the night before, seen my face and my future. And yet now he didn't recognise me? All of a sudden, I wasn't the slightest bit afraid of him any more.

'Hi,' I said. 'My name is, er . . . Lovecraft. Harry Lovecraft. I'm, umm, here on holiday with, umm, my three big brothers. Back home, miles away, I'm involved with my school newspaper. The teachers always encourage us to find interesting things to write about and I thought perhaps I could write about you.'

His sharp green eyes scanned my face like laser beams. He was obviously trying to work out all he could about me.

'I'm sorry, Mr Lovecraft,' he said. 'I do not give interviews.'

'It'd be great publicity,' I said. 'When all my friends read about what a great magician you are —'

He leaned forward suddenly, glaring. A shivering feeling ran up my back.

'I am not a magician, boy,' he snarled. 'I am gifted with second sight. I am a means by which the departed may communicate with the living.'

'But you do a stage act,' I said. 'Surely that means —'

'My public performances are the only way I can make my way in this world, boy. You do not understand.' He sat back on his sofa, his face wreathed in shadows and smoke. 'The dead speak to me, at all hours they whisper in my mind. I am locked in eternal struggle with the spirit realm. My soul is held in the chill fingers of the grave. I cannot lead a normal life, I exist only for the voices. I am compelled to use my gifts in their service, to bring their words to the living. My appearances upon the stage are no act. They are my only means of fulfilling my destiny.'

'I see,' I said, hoping that my voice was shuddering less than the rest of me. 'Well, why not put the record straight? Let me write an article about you and everyone will know that you're a real, genuine, honest psychic.'

Mr Frye became still and silent once more. 'I do not give interviews. I require a period of quiet contemplation before a performance. You will leave me now.'

'Oh well,' I said cheerily. 'Just let Uncle, er, Mr Moustique know if you change your mind. See ya!'

I headed for the door. On the way, I couldn't help noticing a pile of local newspapers that sat in a teetering heap beside Godfrey Frye's sofa. That's odd, I thought, he's only been in town for a matter of days. He must have got every local paper for miles around there. I wonder why.

Chapter Four

I RETURNED TO IZZY. HER mum was returning from the bar, zigzagging her way around the tables. The weirdly dressed man had gone.

'I think the show will be starting in a minute,' said Izzy's mum.

'Mum,' said Izzy. 'You've forgotten our drinks.'

She looked down, as if she was suddenly surprised to find herself not carrying a tray. 'Oh, yes . . . orange juice . . . sorry, I must have got distracted for a moment.'

She turned and zigzagged back to the bar again.

'And some crisps too, please!' called Izzy after her. Her mum waved a hand in acknowledgement.

'Cheese and onion!' Izzy turned to me. 'How did it go?'

'Like a car with no wheels. It didn't go anywhere,' I

said. 'You were right, though, he'd scare the socks off a blood-drinking monster from outer space. At least I've managed to prove to myself that he's no more in touch with the dead than I am.' I told her about him not recognising me.

'That's a relief,' said Izzy. 'The research I've been doing today has been rather comforting, too. There was a lot of info about the history of fake mediums. It makes me see what a fool I was to start wondering if Godfrey Frye was genuine or not!'

'Once I've seen his act and we know how it's done, we can prove to your uncle that because Frye is a fake, this get-rich-quick scheme – whatever it turns out to be – is going to be a waste of time.'

A spotlight pointing at the stage curtains suddenly flashed into life. The point where the curtains met in the middle flapped apart and Izzy's uncle appeared to a round of applause from the audience.

He raised a microphone to his beaming smile. 'Good evening, ladies and gentlemen, boys and girls, and welcome to The Pig and Fiddle. In a short while, we will once again be presenting the master of mysticism, Mr Godfrey Frye. But first, back again by popular demand, the local legends who are . . . The Fat Dads!'

An almighty cheer rose up, as Izzy's uncle scuttled out of the way and the curtains parted. Taking up superstar-shaped poses on the stage was a four-piece band: a drummer, two guitarists and that weirdly-dressed man who'd been at the bar on lead vocals. The rest of the band were dressed even more weirdly than he was, with spiked, multi-coloured hairdos and leather collars around their necks.

The crowd cheered themselves hoarse. I looked around in total bewilderment. I spotted Izzy's mum, back by the bar, jumping up and down and whooping at the top of her voice.

'What on *earth* is this?' I shouted to Izzy above the din of the crowd.

'The Fat Dads. They're a punk-rock tribute band,' shouted Izzy above the sudden clashing of electric guitars. 'They're a local group – they play here quite regularly. The lead singer there is called Jimmy. He and Uncle Raphael go way back.'

The band was bashing out a song which appeared to be called 'Zurp Yar Dweebo Deeba'. Izzy and I were obviously the only ones who weren't loving every second of it. Izzy's mum was now leaping from side to side and clapping along with the beat.

'Your mum's quite keen on them, then?' I yelled.

'I'm afraid so,' yelled Izzy.

'She knows Jimmy too, does she? Since she was chatting to him?'

'Everyone knows Jimmy,' howled Izzy. 'And Jimmy knows everyone. He's the nosiest person I've ever met, always gossiping. Even so, he's best buddies with half the town. Don't like him, personally. Rather full of himself.'

The band played for about half an hour. I could see why they'd called themselves The Fat Dads. They were all in their forties and they all had bellies hanging over the tops of their trousers like froth overflowing from a coffee cup.

'He's Mrs McEwan's brother, you know,' shouted Izzy.

'What, Mrs McEwan our school secretary?' I bellowed.

'Yup. She tells him all about the cases you solve at school. Every time he sees me he wants to hear more stories about you. Nosy, like I said.'

The band finished their set with a five-minute series of chords and wails. The audience clapped and cheered as the four of them took half a dozen bows and bounded off backstage.

As the crowd settled down again, Izzy's mum came back and plonked herself down between Izzy and me.

'They're such fun, aren't they?' she gasped, out of breath from all that leaping about. I was seeing an entirely new side of Izzy's mother tonight!

'You've forgotten the orange juices again,' said Izzy. 'And the crisps.'

'What?' asked her mum. 'Oh, yes, right. Must have got distracted. Back in a mo.'

'Cheese and onion,' said Izzy.

Off went Izzy's mum again. Uncle Raphael reappeared at the curtains.

'Ladies and gentlemen,' he said, in a deep, serious tone, 'I am now proud to present to you a man whose ability to see beyond this ordinary world of ours is as unmatched as it is mysterious. A man who has a gift which the rest of us can only dream of. A man who can speak . . . directly! . . . to those who have passed on and to whom the spirits speak in turn. Ladies and gentlemen, Mr Godfrey Frye.'

There was a steady ripple of applause, then the crowd became hushed and nervous.

Suddenly, I realised something. I had to move! At once!

'I'll be over on the other side of the room,' I whispered to Izzy. 'I can't let Frye see me sitting here.'

'Why?' whispered Izzy.

Can you see what I was trying to avoid?

If Godfrey Frye saw me sitting next to Izzy (who he'd already met the night before, remember), he'd know that Izzy and I were connected. And if he found that out, he might well realise that I wasn't who I'd said I was. *Then* he might suspect that I was in the process of investigating him. And *then* he might twig that I was this Saxby Smart person he'd obviously heard about.

I hurried away from the stage, looking for someone who might pass as . . . what was it I'd said to Godfrey Frye? Three big brothers, wasn't it? Oh bum, why couldn't I just have said I'd run away from home or something?

But I was in luck. Three hefty blokes in builder's overalls were huddled around a table close to the toilets. All three of them looked like sausage skins stuffed with pebbles, and all three of them gave me a 'get lost' look as I approached.

'Do you mind if I sit here?' I said breezily. 'You get a much better view from, um, near the toilets, don't you.'

They stared at me. 'If you must,' grunted one of them. They paid no more attention to me.

The stage lights dimmed a little. There was absolute silence. I could have sworn a sudden chill rippled its way outwards across the room.

Godfrey Frye walked into the spotlight, his shoes clacking slowly against the stage. Somehow, he looked even more sinister in bright light. He acknowledged the audience with a wearily raised hand.

'I hear a message for a woman named Kate, or Katherine,' he began. Two or three sections of the crowd bristled excitedly. 'This lady has recently suffered a bereavement. Her dear grandmother has passed over into the spirit world.'

A woman sitting close to the bar raised a trembling hand. Her face was fixed on Godfrey Frye, her eyes almost popping out of her head with surprise.

'Would you stand?' said Mr Frye.

The woman stood up and a second spotlight swung around to pick her out of the crowd. Godfrey Frye was silent for a few seconds, standing with his hands raised to his forehead and his eyelids half closed.

'You grandmother's name was Edith,' he said. His words seemed to split the air in the room like a saw carving into wood.

'Y-yes, that's right,' said the woman.

'She has a message for you,' said Godfrey Frye. 'She is telling you . . . not to be sad. She is telling you . . . she is happy in the spirit world . . . and that your family should not worry about her. She says that you must convey this message to your sister Veronica and to your mother Rosalind.'

The woman was almost toppling over with

astonishment. 'I . . . Y-yes, I will,' she cried. 'Thank you. Does she say anything else?'

Godfrey Frye paused. His head shifted slightly to one side, as if he was concentrating on a sound that was echoing from far away. 'Yes,' he said. 'She sees your future. I am shown . . . is it an office? No, a shop, perhaps? No, something else . . . There are boxes and . . . envelopes . . .'

'That's where I work!' cried the woman. 'At the sorting depot. I work for the Post Office!'

'Your future contains a great success,' said Godfrey Frye. 'The spirits are showing me . . . a promotion? A change of job?'

The woman gasped. 'I know what that means! Thank you, yes, I know what that means! I've been thinking about applying for a supervisor's job! Now I know I should go for it!'

'Then I am glad the spirits have been able to help you,' said Godfrey Frye. He nodded to the crowd and they clapped wildly.

'Wait,' he said. The crowd instantly hushed. 'The spirits are also showing me great success for someone else here in this room. Success with money. For someone who is . . .' His fingers waivered in front of his forehead and his eyelids fluttered. 'Who is . . . a member of a large family, someone very popular and . . . I am being shown . . . I believe it is our own Mr Raphael Moustique.'

The audience whispered approvingly. Izzy's uncle, now standing behind the bar, perked up at the mention of his name. Suddenly, Godfrey Frye breathed deeply and lowered his hand, as if his connection to the undead has just been broken.

'No, ladies and gentlemen, I'm afraid the spirits will allow me no more of that vision. Even I cannot predict what they will reveal.' The audience chuckled. 'So, let us move on . . . I am now seeing a faithful, much-loved companion . . . A dog, named . . . is it Keith? Kenneth? . . .'

There was a gasp of joy from a table close to me. 'That's Killer!' cried an old man, waving his hands in the air. 'Oh, dear little Killer!'

It turned out that Killer was very happy in the afterlife, that he had all the rabbits he could eat and that his ex-owner would soon find happiness with a lady whose name began with T.

For almost an hour, Godfrey Frye 'talked' to the dead. He correctly told a woman in a red dress all about the house she'd recently inherited and predicted that next spring would be a good time to sell it. He held a man's pocket watch and correctly gave us its history, then informed the man that his long-gone grandfather wanted to make sure the watch stayed in the family for ever. He found a couple in the audience for whom the number 247 was significant, correctly diagnosed their dead relative's final illness and let them know that their dead relative was telling them to switch to a low-fat diet.

I still couldn't quite work out *how* he was doing it.

However, I *was* getting angry. Partly at all those in the audience who were taking him seriously and partly at Frye himself. This guy was preying on these people's most sensitive feelings. He was suckering them into believing everything he said by trapping them in a skilful mish-mash of facts and lies, like a spider trapping bugs.

And he was very, *very* good at it. Once or twice, I even caught *myself* wondering what these dead people were going to advise their still-living family members!

After a few more chats from beyond the grave, Godfrey Frye announced that the spirits had exhausted him. Tonight's contact with the realm of the mysteries was at an end. Thank you for your attention, ladies and gentlemen, blah blah blah.

He left the stage to thunderous applause. As soon as he'd gone, the chill seemed to lift and everyone started behaving normally again. I went back to Izzy's table. Her mum had finally returned and was sitting next to her.

It was now time to take action and find out what this get-rich-quick scheme of Izzy's uncle's actually was. He told Godfrey Frye he'd talk to him after the show. I had to listen in! Somehow . . .

'He's really unnerving, that Godfrey Frye, isn't he?' said Izzy's mum. 'So accurate. I'm still wondering if he's for real?'

'Muuuum,' said Izzy crossly. 'You've forgotten the orange juice again. And the crisps. Again.'

'Oh. Watching that Godfrey Frye must have distracted me,' said her mum. 'Anyway, it's too late now. We've got to be going. You two have got school tomorrow.'

'Before we go,' I said quickly, 'I need to have a word with Izzy's uncle.'

'What about?' said Izzy's mum.

I tried to think of something that wouldn't give away the fact that I wanted to spy on his meeting with Godfrey Frye. 'Um . . . my next door neighbours. They have a really great stage act. They do, um —'

'Juggling,' said Izzy, at exactly the same moment I said, 'Trampolining.'

'Juggling on a trampoline?' said Izzy's mum. 'I'll look forward to seeing that! OK, I'll wait here. Don't be long!'

I headed back towards Frye's room and Izzy followed me. 'You see what I mean?' she whispered.

'Yes,' I said, 'he's scarily effective, isn't he? Mind you,

I think people just *want* to believe it's true. I suppose it's kind of reassuring to think your dead relatives are still taking an interest.'

'The important thing is to present my uncle with a cast-iron case,' said Izzy. 'Prove Frye is a phoney. How are we doing on that score?'

'Er, not very well,' I said. 'We have nothing yet which would change his mind, I'm sure.'

'Maybe we could trick Frye somehow?' suggested Izzy. 'Do you think we could get him to admit it's all trickery? Perhaps we could even secretly *record* an admission.'

I shook my head. 'He's too good. He won't let his guard down. I should think he's so used to playing the mystic he almost believes it himself. He'd only tell the truth to someone he really needed to.'

We reached the corridor outside Frye's room. His door was wide open. The pong of cigarette smoke was still hanging thickly inside the room, but Frye himself was nowhere to be seen.

I quickly glanced up and down the corridor. 'Shout if anyone turns up,' I whispered.

Before Izzy could object, I nipped inside the room. Izzy let out a squeak of alarm, but stayed put on guard.

I probably had a matter of seconds. Godfrey Frye wouldn't have left his door open if he was planning on being gone for more than a minute or two. Quick, quick, look for clues!

There wasn't much in the room that might have even *been* a clue. Apart from the sofa, a small table and chair with a mirror on the wall beside it, the place was almost empty. There was a tall, curtained window, and hanging up in a long line were a series of framed photographs of various stage acts shaking hands with Izzy's uncle and grinning. There didn't seem to be anything at all in the room that was personal to Godfrey Frye.

Suddenly, I heard a sharp 'Psssst' from Izzy in the doorway. I turned, but she'd already ducked out of sight. The sound of slow footsteps was coming along the corridor.

There was no way I could leave the room without being seen. In a panic, I dived behind the sofa. I lay there with my knees pulled up, and my head level with the arm of the sofa nearest the window.

I heard the door shut softly. The footsteps crossed the room. My heart was thumping away faster than the drummer in The Fat Dads.

The sofa suddenly shuddered and billowed as someone dropped heavily on to it. Then I heard the sharp sound of a match being struck and a few seconds later a fresh cloud of cigarette smoke wafted through the air. I fought back the urge to cough.

A hand dropped down to the side of the sofa, just centimetres from my face. A hand with claw-like bony fingers. That pile of local newspapers I'd spotted before was right in front of my nose. The hand grasped the top one and lifted it out of sight.

Trying not to move, I peeped at the remaining newspapers. They were in an untidy heap and I noticed that all of them – well, all the ones I could see, anyway – were folded back at one particular page. These pages showed different issue dates at the top, but they were all headed *Obituaries*. I shuddered slightly. This guy was *reading* about dead people, now, not just talking to them!

There was a loud knocking at the door. I almost jumped out of my skin, but luckily Godfrey Frye's shifting on the sofa covered up whatever sudden twitch I might have made.

'Mr Frye?' came Uncle Raphael's voice from outside. 'Might I have that chat with you now?'

On the one hand, I was delighted: I was going to get a ringside seat at this meeting and not miss a word of it. On the other hand, I was terrified: I was trapped behind this sofa and I had no idea what might happen if I was discovered.

'You may enter,' drawled Godfrey Frye. His voice

sounded even more rasping and sinister than usual.

The door opened and Raphael bustled in, bumping it shut behind him. 'Wonderful show this evening, Mr Frye. Wonderful. I was so deeply moved.'

'Thank you,' said Godfrey Frye.

Twisting my arm around carefully, I fetched my trusty notebook from my pocket. Pen at the ready, I scribbled down the entire conversation. Here's a copy of what they said, including a couple of extra notes in brackets:

Raphael: I've got a little business proposal for you, old bean.

Frye: I do not have much money at my disposal, Mr Moustique. If you're expecting me to invest in some new venture of yours, then I'm afraid that —

Raphael: Ooooh, no no no, nothing like that. This is something entirely unique. This is an idea of mine that you, and you alone, are the key to. It requires your own very special talents to even make it possible, old chap.

Frye: I don't understand.

Raphael: Mr Frye, your gift of second sight is nothing short of amazing. Y'know, I wasn't sure that such things really existed until now. You've proved to me that I was right to keep an open mind. I said to myself only this morning, I said, Raffie, I said, it is fate that has brought Mr Godfrey Frye and you together. Sheer good luck, as it were, that we can . . .

(Handwriting scribbled so fast, can't read this bit.)

Frye: But what is it that you are proposing? How is it that I can help you?

(Behind sofa, S. Smart's eyes are watering from the cigarette smoke. Really needs to cough!)

Raphael: How do you fancy winning a small fortune?

Frye (Long pause): In what way?

Raphael: By entering into a little game of chance. I'm not a betting man, myself, you understand. In fact, the entire gambling scene is quite repugnant to me. But this is a highly unusual situation. You see, we have an American chap arriving at this hotel in two days' time. From America. I happened to take his booking myself and got chatting. Very interesting man. He's a professional poker player. He gambles for a living.

Frye: Really? Such a profession must be even less profitable that working on the stage!

Raphael: My thought exactly! But this American, it turns out, has just had a collosal stroke of good fortune. He's won umpteen thousands of dollars and he's treating himself to a holiday over here by way of celebration.

Frye: Surely you don't intend to play this man at cards?

Raphael: Not MYSELF, no, no. My idea is for YOU to play him at cards.

Frye: I'm sorry, it's out of the question. I know nothing about card games, I've never played poker in my life, and in any case I simply don't approve of gambling.

Raphael: Ah, but, y'see, it's not really gambling, as such, really, now, is it? Not when you know where every card in the deck is.

(Long pause. Silence. S.Smart *really* needs a good cough!)

Frye: Mr Moustique, are you suggesting that I should use my powers to cheat at cards?

Raphael: Oh, not cheat, no no no, it's not cheating. It would simply be using your natural talents. He uses his natural talents as a card player, you'd use your natural talents as a psychic. The spirits would be able to show you every card he plays. Before he even plays it!

Frye: That is an outrageous misuse of my gifts. I'm sorry, Mr Moustique, but the answer is no. Besides, as I have told you, I do not have much money at my disposal.

Raphael: No, but I do. Just at the minute, I have access to quite a large sum . . .

(The Big Holiday Fund Izzy mentioned!)

Raphael: . . . Think of it! My cash, your psychic abilities. We could bet every last penny I possess and be sure of winning. We'd make a mint, an absolute stack of dosh!

Frye: Have you not been listening? The answer is no. Now, good night, Mr Moustique. I require considerable rest after the trauma of the evening's performance.

(Frye gets up off sofa and heads for door.)

Raphael: Surely there's some way I can persuade you . . .?
Frye: There is not. I will not insult the spirits by making a profit out of them!
Raphael: But you take fees from me for your performances. What's the difference?
Frye: A fee for my services is unfortunately necessary. I need to make a living, somehow. But taking a share of winnings, gained through my contact with the spirits, that is something entirely different.
Raphael (Slapping his hands together in glee): Well, then, that's the solution! I'll give you a flat fee. For services rendered, 'n' all that. You play this American, using my money and afterwards I pay you a simple fee. Call it a bonus, for all the extra customers you've been bringing to The Pig and Fiddle this last week, eh? How does that sound? You won't be touching the profits, as such.
Frye (Long pause): What sort of fee?
Raphael: Well now, let's see. How does two thousand pounds grab you?
(Behind sofa, S. Smart almost drops notebook.)
Frye: I would still be risking the anger of the spirits. They might extract some penalty from me . . . I'll take no less than ten thousand pounds.
(Behind sofa, S. Smart almost drops notebook again.)
Raphael: Three thousand.

Frye: Nine.

Raphael: Four.

Frye: Eight.

Raphael: Five.

Frye: I'll accept six, provided I have a signed contract, which guarantees me the money. No matter what.

Raphael: It's a deal! Splendid! I'll have that contract for you in the morning! Fancy a drinkie, on the house, for free, my shout?

Frye: Thank you, no. I must get back to my rented rooms on the other side of town.

(Door opens. Both step out into corridor.)

Raphael: Righty-ho! And, ah . . . mum's the word, eh? Not a word to a living soul. We, ah . . . never had this conversation, wink wink, eh?

Frye: I understand entirely, Mr Moustique.

As soon as they'd gone, I scurried out of my hiding place and raced back to Izzy and her mum in the pub. Well, first I had a good cough, *then* I scurried back to Izzy and her mum in the pub.

'What happened?' gasped Izzy, wide-eyed.

'I'll tell you in the car,' I said. 'You will not believe it.'

'Oh, there you are at last, Saxby,' said Izzy's mum. 'Come on, time to go.'

The night air out on the street was cool, breezy and

fresh-smelling. Izzy's mum had parked a short distance away and I was looking forward to the walk, to clear the smog out of my poor, suffering lungs.

We passed the narrow alleyway that ran between The Pig and Fiddle and the first of the houses next door. As we did so, something suddenly caught my eye – a brief flash of light.

Keeping out of sight around the corner of the building, I peered into the darkness. There it was again! The night breeze must have blown the first match out. There was Godfrey Frye, striking a second match to light a cigarette. The yellowy flash lit up his face for a second or so. And I could see that there was someone with him. They were talking together in hushed tones.

I couldn't quite make out who it was Frye was talking to. The flash of the match only revealed a wild-haired shape, which . . .

I suddenly realised it was Jimmy, the singer with The Fat Dads. And in that instant, several things slotted together in my mind.

'Saxby!' called Izzy's mum. 'Don't dawdle! It's getting late!'

I hurried to catch up. 'I've got it!' I said to Izzy. 'I know how Godfrey Frye is finding stuff out about people! I know how he comes out with all those spookily accurate facts!'

It all revolved around two things. Can you work out what they were? (You'll have to wait till the next chapter to see if you're right.)

A Page From My Notebook

OK, let me get this straight: Izzy's uncle is going to use a FAKE medium to play a REAL gambler.

Obvious conclusion: Raphael is going to lose every last penny of that Big Holiday Fund. What a twit!

Wait a minute! If Frye loses the game, as he will, because he can't REALLY get messages from the dead to tell him what cards are where, then . . . What's in it for him?

Wait a minute part 2! Remember his deal with Raphael. A contract! Raphael has agreed to pay Frye the money whatever happens. Frye doesn't NEED to win! Raphael is going to end up owing money to this American gambler AND to Frye! What a twit!

Think, think, think. What was it Frye said? 'I would still be risking the anger of the spirits. They might extract some penalty from me.' Of course! He's being really clever. He knows perfectly well he'll never beat an experienced card player. So, when he loses, he's now got a ready-made excuse: Oooh dear, the spirits didn't like it. Oooh dear, they gave me the wrong messages, ever so sorry about that, deary deary me. Can I have my money now, please. Then Raphael is forced to pay up. WHAT! A! TWIT!

What to do next: Demonstrate to Raphael how Frye is able to gather his information. Raphael simply CAN'T carry on with his scheme once he knows Frye is a fake. He just CAN'T. Can he?

Chapter Five

By the end of school the next day, I'd told Izzy all about my conclusions. Then she'd done a bit of forehead slapping and a bit of 'why didn't I think of that'-ing. Then she'd phoned her uncle and arranged for the two of us to go over to The Pig and Fiddle as soon as lessons were finished to talk to him and her cousins and anyone else who'd listen.

On the way over, Izzy handed me a set of printouts.

'I did some checking in the IT suite at lunchtime,' she said. 'You need a licence to run a place like The Pig and Fiddle. If my uncle starts allowing gambling to go on, he'll probably lose that licence and be in a lot of trouble on top of that. If the police discover what he's planning, it's game over. Literally.'

'You think that'll be enough to persuade him to call this whole thing off?' I said.

'No way,' huffed Izzy. 'He's so convinced his scheme's going to work, he'll think it's worth the risk.'

'If the police mustn't find out about this,' I said, 'then we won't let on that *we* know about his scheme. Let's keep it as quiet as possible. We'll simply concentrate on exposing Frye as a fake, OK?'

'Good idea,' said Izzy. 'That way, once we've made my uncle see the truth about Frye, he'll cancel the game himself. That way he'll think it was all his idea. He's stubborn as well as gullible, remember.'

Things were looking worse and worse for Izzy's uncle. And once the Big Holiday Fund was gone, they'd look pretty miserable for Izzy's aunt and six cousins too!

By half past four that afternoon, Izzy and I were perched on stools in The Pig and Fiddle's pub section, facing the bar and an assortment of people: there was Izzy's uncle, the restaurant's head chef (a skinny, ginger-haired man who was also convinced that Godfrey Frye was genuine) and Izzy's six cousins, who ranged in age from early twenties down to about five.

'This,' said Izzy, pointing to each in turn, 'is Coral, Jade, Sapphire, Ruby, Pearl and Emerald.'

'Hello, cousins,' I said. They waved.

There were a handful of customers in the pub, mostly sitting towards the other side of the room. None of them took much notice of what I was saying.

'OK,' I announced. 'Let's talk about Godfrey Frye. Or rather, let's talk about, er, let's see now, you, Coral.'

Coral was the eldest, a tall young woman with a tapering face, wearing a kitchen apron. She did a comical 'Ooh, me?' gesture.

I became very serious. I closed my eyes and allowed my features to freeze in concentration. I held my hands to the sides of my head. 'You are planning a journey. I see a green car, with . . . something on the passenger seat. No, it's a rip in the fabric. Taped over. I see . . . is it a pet? It's a toy, a little toy nodding dog, sitting on the car's dashboard. It came from . . . a Christmas cracker. The green car is . . . being driven by a man with a scar on his arm. His name begins with a J. Is it James? No, it's John. You are travelling towards . . . music?'

I opened my eyes. Coral was staring at me, open-mouthed. 'How the bloomin' heck did —?'

Emerald, the youngest cousin, tutted loudly. 'Izzy must have told him, dum-dum.'

Coral shook her head as if clearing out cobwebs. 'Blindlingly obvious. Why didn't I see that instantly?'

'Because I dressed it up in all that mind-reading rubbish, that's why,' I said. 'You weren't expecting me to come out with that, so you took what I said at face value. Izzy told me about you and your boyfriend going to a rock festival next month and I simply muddied up the details a bit.'

Uncle Raphael cleared his throat noisily. 'Yes, good trick 'n' all that, but what does this have to do with Godfrey Frye, young man?'

'You *really* don't know?' gasped Izzy.

'Suppose someone bumped into you in the street,' I said to Uncle Raphael. 'Someone you'd never met. A complete stranger. And instead of simply apologising and walking on, they suddenly started saying that the instant you bumped into them they'd had a psychic glimpse into your mind. What if that person could immediately reel off information about you? What if they could describe where you live? What if they then claimed they could follow your life into the future? What would you think about that?'

'I'd be amazed and astounded!' declared Uncle Raphael. 'And so would you be, young man!'

'Exactly,' I said. 'But if that happened to you, which is the more reasonable explanation? That they read your mind? *Or*, that they'd found out about you *in advance*?'

'You can't dismiss the psychic arts as trickery,' bumbled Uncle Raphael. 'To quote Hamlet, *There are more things in heaven and earth —'*

'Yesyesyes,' I said. 'I'm not saying that *all* out-of-the-ordinary things are rubbish. They need proper, scientific investigation. What I'm saying is that they're open to trickery and they're *certainly* open to trickery in the case of Godfrey Frye and his whispers from the dead.'

'I'm afraid that really doesn't wash,' chuckled Raphael. 'Godfrey Frye's been abroad for years. He doesn't know anyone in this area. There's no way he could find out information about people in advance.'

'There are two ways; he has two sources of information,' I said. 'Number one. The local news-papers. More specifically, the local obituaries. It's perfectly easy to find out the names of people in the area who've died recently and some other names and facts associated with them. Just read all the obituaries. Then, bingo, you can produce the names of dead relatives as if by magic.'

'You're barking up the wrong tree.' Uncle Raphael smiled, clearly amused. 'You couldn't possibly link up what you'd read in obituaries with the random people who turn up in an audience to see your act.'

'Ah!' I said. 'That's where source number two comes in. Number two is Jimmy, the singer with The Fat Dads. He's the local gossip. He knows everyone around here and everyone knows him. He'd be perfect for supplying Godfrey Frye with *all kinds* of information. About who's in the audience, about what connections there are between different people, about *endless* things that are going on.'

'Are you suggesting that my old pal Jimmy is in league with Godfrey Frye to pull the wool over everyone's eyes?' exclaimed Uncle Raphael.

'Yes!' I cried. 'What Godfrey Frye is doing has been standard practice for fake mediums since Victorian times!'

'He's right,' said Izzy. 'It's all in my research. Nineteenth century mystics used to go to amazing lengths to find out stuff. They'd also set up incredibly elaborate tricks to make it look like spirits were in the room.'

'But not my friend Jimmy,' said Uncle Raphael, sounding slightly hurt. 'We've known each other for years. He's a mate.'

'He's also a stage performer,' I said. 'Just like Godfrey Frye. He's no fool. He'll be well aware of just how these things work. Godfrey Frye will have turned up in this town deliberately looking for someone like Jimmy. The local know-it-all, the local everyone's-friend. You find them wherever you go. All Frye has to do is sneakily get Jimmy on his side, possibly even pay him for info, and all of a sudden he's got loads of personal facts at his fingertips. Think about it. All Jimmy's got to do is take a good look around a crowded pub and he can pick out a couple of dozen people he knows, or more. He tells Frye who they are, and what he knows about them. If he strikes lucky, Frye can cross-reference that info with stuff he's got from the obituaries. If not, then any audience will still contain people who've lost *some* relative at *some* time. And ta-daa, Frye can go on stage, claim he's talking to the dead and produce true facts about people in the audience.'

Raphael sighed and shook his head. 'No, no, no. Godfrey Frye's results have been more impressive than that. He knows so *much* about people. If you were going to pull off a trick in that way, you'd have to gather absolutely vast oodles of data. Tonnes of it.'

'But this is the guy's *job*,' I said. 'He's got a very strong motive to gather absolutely vast oodles of data. The trick is in using information cleverly.' I had a sudden thought. 'Aha! He picked out Izzy, the other night! Perfect example! There you are, he had information about Izzy and her mum and so he picked them out and started doing his mystic bit on them!'

'But I've never spoken to him about Izzy,' said Uncle Raphael.

'Nooooo,' I said, sliding my hands down my face in frustration. 'He got it all from *Jimmy*. Izzy's mum and

Jimmy know each other. They were yattering together for ages last night.'

'That was how Frye knew about Saxby,' said Izzy. 'Mum had talked to Jimmy about him. Jimmy told Frye. Frye heard "spirits" talking about him in front of me. Although, actually, I'm still not sure why.'

'That's easy,' I said. 'Frye's a fake. He's heard I'm a brilliant schoolboy detective. He doesn't want any brilliant schoolboy detectives nosing around, revealing his methods, does he? So what does he do? He makes sure that you, Izzy, a friend of this detective, get told that there's failure and disaster in my future.'

'To scare you?' said Izzy. 'To put you off going anywhere near him? To make others doubt your deductions?'

'Exactly,' I said. 'He didn't know how much of a threat I'd be to him. So he played safe and tried to warn me off. Hah! Well, he didn't reckon on who he was dealing with, did he? He didn't reckon on Saxby Smart!'

The moment I stopped speaking, I noticed that everyone in front of me was staring glumly over my shoulder.

'So,' said a slow, scratchy voice behind me, 'you are the detective I've been hearing about, eh? Not Mr Lovecraft after all?'

I turned, a prickling sensation creeping along the back

of my neck. The bar stool creaked beneath me.

Godfrey Frye was standing less than a metre away. His creased, parchment face loomed over me.

I flashed him a cheesy grin. 'Hello,' I said weakly.

'Good afternoon to you, Mr Frye,' cried Uncle Raphael, scuttering out from behind the bar and skipping over to him like an eager puppy. 'Saxby here has been quite the theatrical critic.' He laughed, too long and loud.

'Indeed,' said Godfrey Frye. 'I've never received quite such a cutting review. I'm glad I only heard the end of it.'

Uncle Raphael laughed again, and again it was too long and too loud. The cousins and the restaurant chef seemed to have vanished into thin air. Izzy was looking sheepish.

'How was the remainder of your evening yesterday, after our little head-to-head, as it were, Mr Frye?' gushed Uncle Raphael. 'And I trust today has been a restful one?'

'Thank you, yes,' said Godfrey Frye. 'The spirits have allowed me some peace since breakfast time.'

'Splendid, splendid,' said Uncle Raphael.

I thought about the way Godfrey Frye had been so cold-heartedly fooling people with his stage act. There was no way I was going to let the likes of him scare me. I gave a sort of half-huff, half-snort.

'Do you have a cold, Mr Smart?' said Godfrey Frye.

'No, I'm snorting with derision,' I said. 'Spirits, eh?'

'I have encountered many sceptics during my years of contact with the departed,' said Mr Frye with an icy smile. 'I have yet to meet one whom I could not convince in the end.'

'Well, you have now,' I said. 'I'm sorry, but it's all trickery. And quite simple trickery, at that.'

'You accuse me of deception and yet you lied to me about your identity,' said Mr Frye. 'Which one of us is the trickster?'

Uncle Raphael laughed so long and loud I thought he might burst a blood vessel. 'Let's leave Saxby and my niece to their own devices, shall we? If you'd like to follow me, Mr Frye, I have your contract ready with regard to the, ahh, business matter we discussed yesterday.'

'But Uncle Raphael!' cried Izzy. 'Have you not listened to what Saxby's said? Haven't we proved to you that Godfrey Frye's stage act is just that? An act?'

Raphael shuffled uncomfortably on the spot. His gaze flicked around the room, resting everywhere except on us and Godfrey Frye. 'Not at all. You've shown me how *you* would *pretend* to have Mr Frye's psychic abilities, but Mr Frye himself has clearly demonstrated to audiences, in public, night after night, on that stage over there, that his skills bring wonder and joy to all who witness them. And that's good enough for me.'

Godfrey Frye took a step towards me. His piercing eyes glared into mine. It took every bit of self-control I had not to look away.

'Young people show such a lack of trust these days,' he hissed. 'Such a lack of faith. It's quite disappointing, quite upsetting.'

'Come along, then, old chap,' said Uncle Raphael to Godfrey Frye. He began to lead Frye away, his arms waving this way and that, as if Frye was a bad-tempered goose that might wander off at any moment.

'The, er, special event I mentioned,' he said, as they moved away towards the backstage corridor. 'It's scheduled for tomorrow night, at ten.'

'You've spoken to Mr Green?' said Godfrey Frye.

'I called him late last night,' said Raphael. 'It was only early evening over there, of course, because of the time difference. I told him about my idea and he was very keen, very keen. He arrives later today.'

They vanished from sight, Raphael still herding Godfrey Frye like a nervous shepherd.

'Right, that's it,' muttered Izzy. 'We have to tell my uncle we know what he's planning. There's no other way now.'

She hopped off her stool. I grabbed her arm before she

could chase after him.

'Wait!' I said. Then I said 'wait' again, because no other words would squeeze out of my brain.

I was staring into mid-air. If I'd been able to drop-stretch my lower jaw to the ground with a mighty clang, I definitely would have.

'Good grief,' I gasped, finally. 'This whole case. I've got it completely wrong. I've been looking at it back to front the entire time!'

'What do you mean?' said Izzy.

I gawped at her. 'Your uncle is not the one who's set this situation up.'

'But this card game was his idea,' said Izzy.

I shook my head slowly. 'Oh no it wasn't. Godfrey Frye's been behind it all along. What's more, Frye is in league with this American gambler, this Mr Green. Frye and Green are in it together, to con your uncle out of all that money.'

'But how do you know?' said Izzy.

Hurriedly, I took out my notebook to check that I was right. I read through yesterday's conversation between Uncle Raphael and Godfrey Frye, the one I wrote down behind the sofa.

'A couple of minutes ago,' I said, snapping my notebook shut again, 'Godfrey Frye said something which gave himself away. Your uncle didn't spot it, but I did.'

'What was it?'

It was only a small detail. But it was something Frye couldn't have said, unless he and the American were working as a team.

Have you spotted it too?

'Frye mentioned the American gambler by name,' I said. 'He referred to him as Mr Green. But your uncle had never told him what this man was called. Last night, he only mentioned that the gambler was an American. And he hasn't spoken to Frye since last night, as was clear when Frye came in just now.'

'I see what you mean,' said Izzy. 'Frye must know who this Mr Green is.'

'Why didn't I see it earlier?' I cried. 'This is a deliberate con. Frye travels around doing his psychic act. Quite often, he'll come across daft suckers who believe he's genuine. Now and again, he'll come across a daft sucker who also has a pile of cash.

'At which point, he alerts his friend, Mr Green. Mr Green comes along, as if by coincidence, and just happens to let slip to Daft Sucker With Money that he's a professional gambler. At which point, Daft Sucker With Money thinks to himself, a-ha, I've got a clever idea.

'Ahhhggh! Frye must have been delighted when he met your uncle. The Pig and Fiddle is the perfect set-up for a con like this. A theatrical venue, attached to a hotel. These two con men make Daft Sucker With Money think it's all *his* idea, so when it all goes belly-up, he doesn't even realise he's been conned. Frye has his ready-made excuse for losing – ooooh-er, the spirits were angry – and Green just has to nip in, win the money and nip out again.'

'So Green will be cheating anyway,' said Izzy.

'Absolutely,' I said. 'Any card game you like. They can let Daft Sucker With Money pick whatever he wants to play, it won't matter.'

'Right,' said Izzy. 'Now we really can go to Uncle Raphael. We can expose Frye and stop the game from happening.'

I thought for a moment. 'No. We can't do that. Frye and Green – huh, if those really are their names – might have been pulling scams like this for years. If we send Frye packing, he'll only go and start up somewhere else. We have to put them out of business.'

'How? Frye's on to you. Your cover's blown.'

'Er, not sure yet.'

'Shouldn't we just tell the police?' said Izzy. 'On second thoughts, we can't do that either. For one thing, a con man as sharp as Frye might well smell a rat. And for another thing, my uncle might still get into trouble for setting the game up, even if it wasn't really his idea.'

I looked at Izzy. 'There's only one thing for it. We're going to have to cheat better than them.'

Chapter Six

TIME: THE FOLLOWING NIGHT, 9.45 P.M.

Place: Muddy's room.

People: Me, Izzy and Muddy.

'This place is a pigsty,' said Izzy.

'Oi,' said Muddy, 'this is a working workshop. Don't sit there, I need that circuit board!'

'Shhhh!' I hissed. 'I'm trying to tune this monitor in!'

Izzy took out a hanky and dusted a patch of carpet before sitting down. Muddy shovelled a pile of electrical components aside to make room for himself. I adjusted the TV's specially adapted remote control (or the Whitehouse Eye-Viewer X350, as Muddy insisted on calling it) and a slightly furry, slightly discoloured picture filled the screen.

'Who's wearing the badge?' asked Muddy.

'My cousin Coral,' said Izzy. 'We had to let her in on the whole thing. There was no way Saxby or I could be there without raising suspicion.'

The picture on the screen swayed as Coral walked. Muddy's mini-camera was hidden behind the left eye of a smiley-face badge, pinned to her apron. Muddy's mini-microphone was attached to the back of a button on her shirt. Muddy's carefully prepared pack of all-the-same playing cards was tucked into her pocket.

We watched from the smiley badge as Coral walked into the backstage room at The Pig And Fiddle. A small table had been placed in the middle of the room, with a chair at each end. Raphael was in there spraying air freshener to try to disperse the pong of Godfrey Frye's cigarettes.

'Everything set?' said Raphael nervously. His voice sounded tinny through Coral's concealed microphone.

'You're still going to do this, Dad?' said Coral. 'You're still going to cheat this gambler?'

'Oh, for goodness' sake, not one of those gamblers plays fair,' said Raphael. 'I've seen it in the movies. They all cheat. Mr Frye and I will simply be redressing the balance.'

'So two wrongs make a right, now, do they?'

'If you can't say anything constructive, Coral, then don't say anything at all.'

'Does she know about our con?' whispered Muddy.

'Yes,' I whispered, 'but she's under strict instructions not to let on to Izzy's uncle. As far as he's concerned, everything's happening according to plan.'

'Why are we whispering?' whispered Izzy. 'They can't hear us, can they?'

'No,' said Muddy. He produced a big bowl full of crisps. 'Anyone want one?'

'Cheese and onion?' asked Izzy.

'No, Mexican chilli heatwave,' said Muddy.

'Ooh, I've not tried those,' said Izzy.

'Can we shut up and pay attention?' I cried. 'We've got Operation Con The Con Men on the go here!'

There was a lot of swishing about on screen as Coral moved around the room. The picture stabilised as she came to a halt and we could see that Godfrey Frye was arriving.

'Ah, Mr Frye,' said Raphael. 'Do take a seat. Our American friend should be along any moment. Lovely chap, had a long talk with him when he arrived. I must say, he's keen as mustard to play this game. Keen as mustard!'

Frye slowly perched himself on one of the chairs beside the table. 'Is it wise to have one of your daughters present, Mr Moustique?' he said. 'I thought this matter was between ourselves?'

'Oh, no problem, no problem,' bustled Raphael. 'Coral is one hundred and ten per cent trustworthy. She asked me if she could sit in on this. Act as waitress, as it were, fetching a few drinkies, that sort of thing.'

'I see,' said Frye slowly. 'Does Mr Green suspect that I am a person gifted with second sight?'

'Ooh, definitely not, old bean,' said Raphael. 'I've taken down all references to you on the billboards. He thinks you're an old pal of mine. An old pal who fancies himself as a bit of a high roller. He thinks you're going to be a pushover. Everything's top notch, A-1, all systems go.'

Crunch, crunch, crunch.

'Muddy! Put those crisps down!' I said.

'But they're Mexican chilli heatwave, my favourite,' said Muddy.

'I don't care!'

There was more back and forth swishing on the screen. Then a large figure in a light grey, three-piece suit swung into view. He had white hair, a drooping moustache and big, owl-like spectacles.

'Looks like he ought to be serving fried chicken in a bucket,' muttered Izzy. 'Pass the crisps, Muddy.'

'Ah!' came Raphael's tinny cry through the TV's speakers. 'Welcome to our exclusive little soirée, Mr Green! Come in, come in. This is the friend I was telling you about, Mr Godfrey Frye.'

'Hi, delighted to meet you, sir,' said the American, reaching across the table and shaking Frye's limply-offered hand. 'Ray-fee here's told me all about you.' He turned towards the camera, or rather, towards Coral. 'And delighted to meet you, too, miss.'

'Thank you,' said Coral. 'Can I get you a drink?'

'A diet soda, thanks,' said Mr Green.

Coral turned and we could now see a smaller table set up in the corner of the room. On it were various glasses and bottles, plus a shiny metal ice bucket. While Coral poured Mr Green his drink, we listened carefully to what was being said behind us. Er, behind *her*.

'You kindly agreed to a simple, three-deal round of Highball, Mr Green, is that right?' said Raphael.

'Certainly,' said Green. We could hear the chair opposite Frye clunk a little as Green sat down. 'Since you gentlemen are new to the gaming tables, a short, easy game seems like a fair deal.'

'Most considerate,' said Frye.

'Short, but no less exciting!' declared Raphael.

'You said it,' said Green.

Coral turned back to the gaming table and placed a glass on a little round napkin next to Green. As she did so Green produced, from the inside pocket of his jacket, the biggest wad of banknotes you could possibly hold together with one elastic band. He bumped it heavily on to the table in front of him.

('Wow,' murmured Muddy.

'Conned out of a whole string of victims, I reckon,' I said.)

Coral turned in time to see Frye place a similar bundle on his side of the table.

('Double wow,' said Muddy.

'That's the entire Big Holiday Fund, and then some,' murmured Izzy.)

'Winner takes all, huh?' said Green. 'Equal stakes, best of three.'

'Just to remind ourselves of the rules,' said Raphael, his voice trembling in a mixture of gleeful excitement and nervous terror, 'each player splits the deck and takes the card that's then on top. Each player reveals their card. Highest value wins and, as you say, Mr Green, it's best of three. Picture cards count as ten, aces count as eleven. All agreed?'

'Agreed,' said Green.

'Agreed,' said Frye.

Raphael took a pack of cards from his pocket, and cut open the plastic wrapper around them. 'As you can see, gentlemen, we are using a new, unused pack.'

('You're sure Coral's pack has the same design on it?' I whispered.

'Yup,' said Muddy. 'She gave him that pack herself.')

Raphael placed the stack of fifty-two cards in the centre of the table. Frye took out a cigarette and lit it, sending gushes of smoke across the table. Green took the cards and shuffled them in full view, then replaced them in exactly the same spot.

'First round, gentlemen,' said Raphael.

There was a pause. Frye and Green eyed each other across the table.

Green reached over to the cards. Delicately, he lifted a section of the cards off the stack, put them down, then placed the remainder of the deck on top of the ones he'd just removed. Then he took what was now the top card, and placed it in front of him, one hand guarding it.

Frye closed his eyes for a moment. Hearing whispers from the dead, no doubt, about where to split the pack.

He reached over, and did the same thing as Green had done. Now they each had a card face down in front of them.

There wasn't a sound around the table. Or in Muddy's room. Muddy sat with a handful of crisps poised in his mouth.

Green turned over his card. Seven of diamonds.

Frye turned his over. Nine of clubs.

Raphael squeaked with glee. 'Mr Frye wins the first round. Your turn to shuffle the cards, Mr Frye.'

Frye shuffled, and replaced the pack.

Round two.

Green split the deck and chose his card. Frye did the same. He placed his card directly in front of him and adjusted his cigarette, sending another cloud of smoke rolling through the dimmed light in the room.

Green took a sip of his drink. Then he turned his card.

Jack of spades.

Frye turned his.

Two of clubs.

Raphael squeaked with horror. 'M-Mr Green wins the second round,' he burbled. 'Everything depends of round three.'

Frye sat back, a carefully composed look of confusion on his face. He passed a hand woefully across his forehead.

Coral moved around the table. She stood to one side of the table, next to the glass she'd put down for Green.

('That's it,' I muttered to myself. 'Get into position, well done.')

Green grinned up at Izzy's uncle. 'You enjoying this as much as me?'

'Oh, y-yes, you bet, definitely,' stammered Raphael. He kept glancing at Frye. Frye kept avoiding his gaze.

'Here we go, gentlemen,' said Green. 'Winner takes all.'

Green shuffled the deck, for the third and last time. He placed them in the centre of the table.

He cut the deck as before, placed the remainder on top and took the top card.

('Now,' I murmured to myself. 'Now!')

Coral suddenly sneezed. She swung her hand up to her nose, and as she did so, she 'accidentally' tipped Green's glass over. A little fizzing puddle quickly spread across the centre of the tabletop.

With a cry of 'Whoa' she picked the deck of cards up and held it high over the table. Raphael sprang forward, pulling out a handkerchief.

'Oh, you clumsy clot!' he growled as he dabbed the tabletop dry.

'Sorry!' said Coral. 'Sorry everyone! At least I saved the cards from getting wet.'

'No harm done, sweetheart,' chuckled Green. Both he and Frye were keeping a close watch on the cards. She replaced them on the table.

But they'd already missed the important bit. In the split second after the glass had spilled and Coral had lifted the cards, while Green and Frye had taken the briefest of glances down at the fizzing liquid, Coral had swapped the cards from hand to hand, substituting Muddy's all-the-same-card pack for the one they'd been playing with.

('Oh perfect!' I cried. 'She did that absolutely perfectly!')

'I do apologise, gentlemen,' said Raphael hurriedly. He glared angrily at Coral. 'Go over there, stand well back.'

Coral backed off. The substituted stack of cards was sitting on the table.

Now it was Frye's turn to take a card. He split the deck and took the top one.

Green and Frye sat silently for a moment. Raphael wiped his brow with his already-dripping handkerchief.

Casually, Green reached out and flipped his card over.

King of diamonds.

Raphael squeaked with despair. Everything now rested on the turn of this last card, Frye's card. He closed his eyes for a moment.

On the opposite edges of the table sat the two bundles of money. Winner takes all.

Frye's cigarette glowed as he dragged on it. Green eyed him, unblinking and confident.

Frye reached out for his card. His bony fingers hooked underneath it. He lifted it slowly. He turned it over and dropped it to the table top, ready and waiting to see a disasterously low number.

Ace of hearts.

'These crisps are yummy,' said Izzy, taking another handful.

'Yah-hooo!' yelled Raphael. 'I knew you could do it, old chap!' He slapped Frye on the back and scooped up the two bundles of money.

Green jumped to his feet, sending his chair tumbling backwards. 'You blithering idiot, Steve!' he roared at Frye. His accent had suddenly turned Cockney. Then he suddenly realised that he'd let his accent suddenly turn Cockney. And that he'd called Godfrey Frye 'Steve' – his real name, I presumed.

Raphael stared open-mouthed at the pair of them. I think the truth was just starting to dawn on him.

Coral stepped forward. She tapped at the camera hidden in her badge, and spoke to Green and Frye. 'If it's any help in making up your minds about what to do now, this whole thing has been caught on camera.'

Green and Frye looked at her, then at Raphael, then at each other. For a second or two, they looked as if they might do something violent. Then they left, kicking over the table and smashing the now-empty glass against the wall as they went.

Coral twisted the badge round so that her face appeared, huge and distorted, on the screen.

'That went well,' she said, to the three of us in Muddy's room. We cheered and ate the rest of the crisps.

Izzy's uncle took several days to recover from the shock.

The shock of the truth about Green and Frye, the shock of playing the game and the shock of finding out that Izzy, Coral and I had saved him from disaster.

What happened to the money? The Big Holiday Fund went straight back into the bank. Izzy persuaded her uncle to donate all the crooks' loot to charity. She persuaded him by saying, 'Unless you do, Aunt Mina's going to hear what you've been up to as soon as she gets back from New Zealand.'

And that, dear readers, is an example of how adults sometimes have to be rescued from their own stupidity.

The morning after the card game, I trotted down to my garden shed, eager to jot down a few notes on the case. Unfortunately, I'd forgotten about the cramped mess I'd left the shed in. As soon as I opened the door, I took one look at it all and groaned.

I thought for a moment. Notes first, tidy up afterwards. Now all I had to work out was how to get to my desk.

Case closed.

Also available

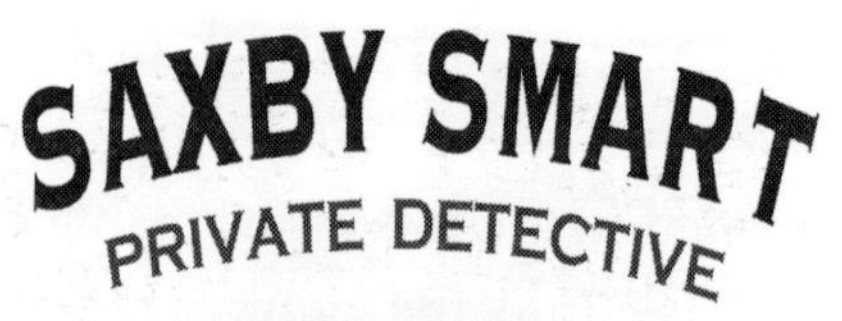

THE CURSE OF THE ANCIENT MASK
and other case files

My name is Saxby Smart and I'm a private detective. I go to St Egbert's School, my office is in the garden shed, and these are my case files.

In this book Saxby solves three of his most puzzling cases: *The Curse of the Ancient Mask, The Mark of the Purple Homework* and *The Clasp of Doom*. In each story Saxby gives you, the reader, clues which help solve the mystery. Are you 'smart' enough to find the answers?

'Talk about being involved in a book! Sharp reads written in a lively and snappy style.' Liverpool Echo

SAXBY SMART
PRIVATE DETECTIVE

THE FANGS OF THE DRAGON
AND OTHER CASE FILES

A string of break-ins where nothing is stolen, a rare comic book snatched from an undamaged safe, and clues apparently leading to a hidden treasure . .

In this book, Saxby Smart - schoolboy detective - solves three more of his challenging cases: *The Fangs of the Dragon*, *The Tomb of Death*. and T*he Treasure of Dead Man's Lane*. In each story Saxby gives you, the reader, clues which help solve the mystery. Are you 'smart' enough to find the answers?

SAXBY SMART
PRIVATE DETECTIVE

A ghostly handprint inside a museum case containing pirate treasure, a new classmate with a mysterious secret, and a strange case of arson in a bookshop . . .

In this third book, Saxby Smart – schoolboy detective – solves three more fascinating cases: *The Pirate's Blood*, *The Mystery of Mary Rogers* and *The Lunchbox of Notre Dame*. In each story Saxby gives you, the reader, clues which help solve the mystery. Are you 'smart' enough to find the answers?

Coming soon

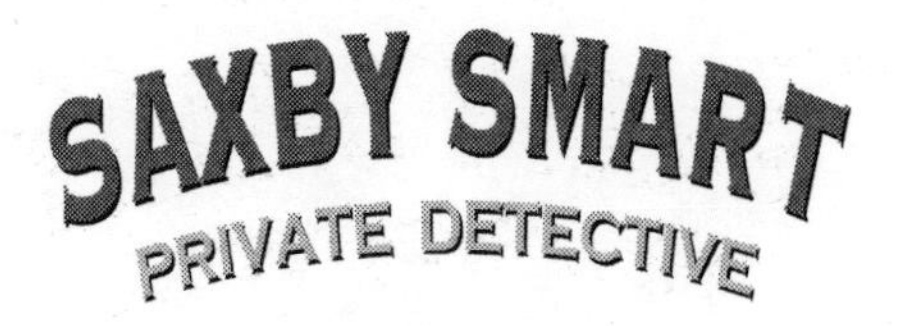

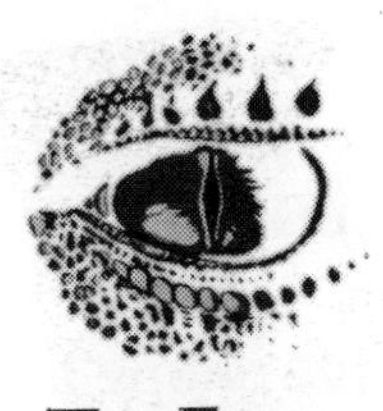

THE EYE OF THE SERPENT

and other case files

Crack three puzzling cases with Saxby Smart: a valuable work of art vanishes into thin air, a notorious crook returns from the dead, and a case of stolen identity.

Saxby Smart – schoolboy detective – returns to unravel three more devious case files, and gives you the clues which solve the mystery. But are you 'smart' enough to work out the answers?

Sign up to Saxby online:

www.piccadillypress.co.uk/saxbysmart.co.uk

- Exclusive online mysteries
- All the latest Saxby news and releases
- Competitions

and much more!

Author Simon Cheshire's personal website can be found at:
www.simoncheshire.co.uk